# The Dasher

## CINDY KEHAGIARAS

CHAMPAGNE BOOK GROUP

The Dasher

This is a work of fiction. The characters, incidents and dialogues in this book are of the author's imagination and are not to be construed as real. Any resemblance to actual events or persons, living or dead, is completely coincidental.

Published by Champagne Book Group
712 SE Winchell Street, Depoe Bay OR 97341 U.S.A.

~~~

First Edition 2023

pISBN: 978-1-959036-77-7



Cover Art by Sevannah Storm



www.champagnebooks.com

Version_1
~~~

Dear Readers:

This book is for those of us in the "Fuck It" time of life. Now go forth my sisters "Mach-Five With Your Hair On Fire" into the next phase of life.

*Cindy*

# **Chapter One**

*Newport Beach, California, 2020*
*Lisa*

I had no idea how long since Uncle Steve stopped talking. The information he'd just given me was still swirling in my head like a tornado picking up speed and sucking everything from my brain into it.

"Lisa, honey. If you intend to sell, some steps must be taken." Uncle Steve's voice was slow and hidden behind an old-fashioned busy signal in my ears, making my head throb.

*Sell Tennent Surf Company? No. Not in my lifetime.*

I rubbed the bridge of my nose, shutting my eyes tight.

My father's oldest friend, not a real uncle, had dropped a bomb on me when I marched into his office. The company was in dire financial trouble, and since no one was taking action, I had to. Uncle Steve was the last person I wanted to see today.

I was already fed up with all the men in my life, but being spoken to like I was six years old, for the hundredth time, was going to make me spontaneously combust. From my runaway father to my indifferent, lazy brother and, finally, my evil ex-husband, they all thought I should go to the spa, get a massage and a pedicure, and let them handle manly stuff. Like running a business. *How's that going, men?*

Not twenty minutes before, sitting in my car heading to beg Uncle Steve for help, I nearly ripped my steering wheel off trying to reach the merchandising contact at Walmart. I had to find out why the annual planning meeting with them hadn't been scheduled, only to be told they weren't renewing our contract for the T-shirts and board shorts we'd produced for them for years.

Tennent Surf Company had one customer in the agreement with Walmart to be the exclusive young men's surf brand for all two hundred-plus stores. My father sold out to the big box retailer to make a crazy amount of money and ensure the name wouldn't be cool again.

"Massimo's making a killing with Target," he'd said to my mother when she'd protested the deal in 2004.

"Do you understand how this part of the business works, sweetheart?" my *uncle* said, tanned and smiling at me with his bright white-capped teeth. "The assets are less—"

"I know what it means." I clenched my jaw and couldn't meet his gaze, fearing that I might launch over his desk and choke him. My hand fell into my lap.

He sat back in his chair with a huff, frustrated with me. "Gus has to sign off on any action."

"I don't know where he is, Uncle Steve," I whined. "He just disappeared."

I tried to hold back the tears from the impossible situation my father had left us in. Tennent Surf Company was sinking fast, and we had no future business since Walmart dropped us.

I'd gone to Dad's house on the cliffs of Laguna Niguel after he hadn't returned my calls for over a week. Ice tingled my scalp at the "For Sale" sign on his front lawn. I'd called the realtor, and she'd been cryptic about when he'd listed it and where in the hell he was.

Taking off wasn't unusual for Gus Tennent. He'd jump on a plane and follow the surf wherever there was a swell: Tahiti, Peru, South Africa, Portugal. He'd be gone for weeks and off the grid with no way to reach him. This vanishing act was beyond his usual antics.

"You can't do anything without his signature. Not even file for bankruptcy." Uncle Steve rolled a shiny pen in his fingers and bobbed in his chair. His silver hair was coiffed perfectly to the right with the blond flecks of the young man he used to be.

"We're past the bankruptcy option." I exhaled slowly.

Tennent was going down like the *Titanic*, and the lifeboat went surfing.

"Not exactly," he said. "Try and cut more overhead. You're hemorrhaging cash, and this won't be able to last long, not without an infusion or an investor."

He took a long inhale through his nose and held it for a second.

"What about Becca? She's invested in the company before and may do it for you and Brad now." Steve crossed his arms over his chest, leaning back in his big leather desk chair. He wore the custom platinum watch on his wrist—one of the gifts Dad had given to his friends with the Tennent logo on it when he'd signed the Walmart deal.

My mother, Rebecca 'Becca' Tennent, had been uncharacteristically silent when I told her Dad was missing. Their marriage had ended twenty years ago, and she harbored vicious feelings about it and him.

She'd say things like, "*He's a stupid surfer who got lucky to find me young and equally as stupid.*" Not that she cared how her daughter had felt about the bile being spewed between her parents.

Sixteen years later, nobody was going to save the company with my father's name.

"She won't help," I said.

My mother was from a wealthy family who'd invested in the development of Irvine, California, as a business haven in the 1980s and owned half of the commercial real estate in Orange County. My brother, Brad, and I even had trust funds once upon a time.

Dad drained those before we had the chance to squander the money at the age of twenty-one like most of our friends had. He'd somehow had the funds transferred to an account with him as the cosigner without us knowing about it and put it into Tennent Surf before the Walmart deal saved the struggling company. *Fucking Uncle Steve* steered that ship for my father.

I considered it my company after my involuntary investment and had to save it.

"So that's it?" I threw my hands up. "I'm totally screwed."

"Let me ask you something that may be hard, and you don't have to answer it right now. Just sleep on it for me, okay?"

I grabbed my purse from the floor beside my chair and held onto it, ready to run, to get out of there and away from Uncle Steve and his smug attitude about my walls crumbling down. Tennent Surf Company was all I had. I'd lost my house, left my husband, misplaced my father, and there was another man in my life telling me not to be emotional.

I clamped onto my bottom lip as the 'F' sound started from my mouth. I wasn't sure what would come out beginning with that letter. It turned out to be two words.

"Fuck. Fine, ask your question," I shouted and clutched my bag, hoping it would pop like a balloon, waking me from this nightmare.

"Would you take on an investor?"

*I would not.*

"Why? So, I can be 'mansplained' *more* on how to run the business and make another cheap deal with JC Penney or Big Lots this time. No, damnit. This brand was the world's leader in cool Southern California surf culture. I will *not* take it down the rag business equivalent of the sewer to make millions of dollars. There will be a renaissance; it's coming. I *will* bring it back."

I stood, still trying to pop my purse, squeezing it so tight something groaned inside. Maybe the Walmart deal ending was a blessing in disguise. Perhaps I could bring the company back from exile? I squeezed tighter.

Snap. *Ugh, now my Gucci sunglasses are broken. How bad can things get?*

"Lisa, be reasonable. You'll need cash and a lot of it."

"I'll find a way." I slung my stupidly expensive Goyard tote bag over my shoulder. "Just find my dad to sign the bankruptcy papers so I can at least get things caught up."

Steve shook his head.

"Please, Uncle Steve." I whimpered.

"I'll put the wheels in motion. You have thirty days to come up with a plan, take on an investor, or find Gus. It's bankruptcy or an investor, Lisa. That's it."

I nodded and opened his office door.

I couldn't come up with a plan except to talk to my mother, despite knowing she wouldn't help. Still, I had to try.

~ * ~

"Men are useless," I grumbled, backing out of the parking space as my convertible top lowered. "Fucking useless."

The curvy canyon drive to my mother's retirement community in Laguna Woods would clear my head. I was going to let my Audi A6 out on that road; the faster, the better. Not giving a fuck who saw me, I shouted along with Limp Bizkit's "Break Stuff" blasting from my stereo.

At the stoplight at Bake Parkway and Lake Forest Drive, I took my emergency stash of Marlboro Lights out of the center console.

After discovering the IVF didn't work for the third time, the hormones had been so severe I had an emotional meltdown. I bought a carton of cigarettes, determined to erode any part of my thirty-nine-year-old body that was still healthy. The pack had been sitting in my car for two years, and I'd only smoked one. Today's bullshit found cause to light up another.

It was David who'd wanted kids. I wasn't sure since my parents had screwed me up so badly. They hated each other and hadn't acknowledged their children's existence for a long time. They'd immersed themselves in the selfish mudslinging during their messy divorce.

Brad and I were caught between them. My parents continued working together for a good ten years after the implosion of their marriage because my mother was the most talented menswear designer on the West Coast.

After Mom graduated from Parson's Design School, she used her trust fund to start their company while Dad was still shaping surfboards and had a respectable following in 1986. The small swim trunk and surfboard company took off when they'd sponsored a seventeen-year-old, good-looking super shredder named Jason Mattis. A local kid with insane talent. It became a global brand, with Jason winning competitions all over the planet.

Mom was a behind-the-scenes design genius, trend forecaster, and marketing master. She'd made Jason the face of the brand with tremendous success. His popularity stole Gus's spotlight. The clothing line grew more significant than Dad's surfboards, and that was when the jealousy started. He wasn't used to being upstaged by anyone, especially not his wife. He couldn't handle being the third fiddle.

Dad took power away from Mom every chance he got, and when Jason retired, they couldn't find the magic again. The brand and the lore of the surf mystique faded in the late 1990s and early 2000s, making the Tennent brand irrelevant and in debt. Hence, Gus's inspiration from his old buddy Massimo to follow his lead and sell his name to a big box retailer. But Walmart? That was the death of cool.

Now, I had to beg Mom to bail out the company.

The drive took shorter than I'd hoped, and before I knew it, I'd smoked two Marlboro's and drove up to the gate of the exclusive retirement community.

I had the key fob to get in since I'd stayed with her for about six months after leaving the house that I had paid half of, decorated, cooked in, slept in, and loved my husband for eleven years. Until I didn't. I just didn't. I didn't cook or sleep or love anymore.

When the IVF hormones took over, I launched a stainless-steel electric teapot at my infuriating husband. I'd missed his head but shattered his first love, his seventy-inch television with the 4K for watching Fox Business News, Chargers football, Angels baseball, Ducks hockey, and UFC fighting every moment he wasn't being a workaholic. I knew then it was time to leave before I physically hurt him or myself.

Why couldn't I get pregnant? Why couldn't I be like the women my age driving an SUV with soccer balls and ice skates in the trunk? Buying healthy lunch-sized snacks at Costco while trying to lose the baby weight and stretch marks?

Those torturous questions made their way into my brain daily. Now, I wondered if it would've made any difference. Having kids wouldn't have saved my marriage. We'd eventually discover we weren't compatible. Then what?

We'd put our kids in the middle of fights and bile-spewing insults, just like my parents. No way. I would preserve whatever sanity I had left and leave him before we ruined more than just our lives.

The familiar smells of eucalyptus and maple trees and the whirring of electric golf carts were almost soothing. I slowed to the speed limit and entered the Laguna Mutual neighborhood with accessible one-story ranch-style houses and the gurgling Aliso Creek nearby.

Mom's house had a shaded courtyard in the front behind a large Maple wood gate. The silver sedan of her caretaker, Maria, sat in the driveway behind Mom's golf cart that she hadn't driven since she broke her hip a few years back. The doctor told her to move into assisted living, but she refused. She didn't care to share space with another human being and had grown accustomed to having things her way. Using the repeated story about going from her parents to the sorority to her husband's house, she liked her independence.

Unlike me, Mom and Brad had many friends. A group of ladies came over to drink Prosecco and play Mahjong with Mom, sloppily driving their drunk, old lady asses home in their matching golf carts.

Mom's real frustration lately was not being able to play golf until she healed. But it was looking like she'd never be able to play ever again.

Maria was leaving with a bundle she'd placed in the trunk of her spotless Hyundai when she opened her arms to me.

"Miss Lisa," she sang and met me at the base of the driveway with a sweet embrace.

I almost started crying at the selfless woman who'd put up with my demanding mother and hugged me like I was one of her own.

She jerked away and crinkled her nose. "You smell like cigarettes. What's wrong?"

She'd told me the tale of her Uncle Paco as a warning when I was staying with Mom.

*Every year for 'Day of the Dead,' they'd place a carton of cigarettes on the rocking chair on the porch, his perpetual spot. He'd smoked three packs of cigarettes a day. His teeth were brown, and his breath smelled. Eventually, he'd lost his ability to talk and sat alone on the porch covered in ashes.*

"I had a couple on the way here. I'm not going to be like Tio Paco, I promise."

She put her hands on my cheeks then jogged to her car, her sizeable rear end bouncing in leggings frayed at the seam. I'd have to talk to Mom about raising Maria's salary to buy clothes.

She produced a mini bottle of Febreze from the center console and a piece of Trident gum from her purse. "Here, take these and wash your hands before you see her."

Selfless, always.

I sprayed all over and handed her the bottle, but she held up a hand in protest. "If you keep smoking, you'll use it. I have others."

I lowered my gum-chewing head like a sassy teenager learning a lesson. "I won't smoke anymore."

"Good," she snapped like the mother of a sassy teenager, making me smile for the first time in what seemed like eons. She left me chomping on my gum and waved as she drove around the corner.

"It's me," I shouted.

Mom's fluffy cat flew from somewhere and, in a blur, scurried down the hallway leading to the bedrooms.

"Oh, honey, I'm in the jacuzzi. Wanna see your naked mother, or can you wait for me to get out?"

I wasn't in the mood to see my naked sixty-five-year-old mother. I doubt I ever would be.

"I'll make tea," I shouted back.

A door opened down the hall just as I found my dented teapot. "Do you have any of that Matcha Toasted Rice left?"

No answer.

I searched the cabinet with thirty boxes of teabags, mostly chamomile and ginger blends, hoping bags of my favorite green tea were left.

When we lived together, she'd gotten me into tea drinking, and I was addicted.

She floated in, her hair wrapped into a white turban towel and matching spa robe with not a wrinkle on her glowing, dewy face. Her high, chiseled cheekbones had a rosy hue, most likely from the heat of the jacuzzi water. My mother was a stunning woman.

"You realize it's almost noon, and you're wearing a robe. It's very lazy of you, Mom," I teased over the steaming mug of turmeric-ginger blend tea.

I heard a tiny wince from her as she brushed past me in the small galley kitchen to reach for the kettle.

"I keep forgetting to take that home with me," I said.

Pouring the water she declared, "Well, it's mine now. Get your own."

She tickled my hip to get out of her way and limped into the living room. I noticed her walking much better than in the months after her surgery. That was my mother; she tried not to let anyone see her out of her perfect existence, even if she was in excruciating pain. Not even me, who'd stayed with her after the surgery when she was bedridden.

Lowering herself onto her beige suede lounger chair with a groan, a motor whirred raising her legs and reclining her. Maxi, her cat, jumped onto her lap, and she lifted her teacup to give the deprived feline room to circle on her lap before committing to lying down.

She stroked the cat and sipped her tea, like Dr. Evil from Austin Powers or the stepmother from Cinderella. I smiled again and sat on the matching couch.

"I saw Uncle Steve this morning," I said, not wasting time.

My mother, Rebecca Tennent, would inherently start her visit with small talk, like the weather or pointless gossip. I wasn't in the mood.

"How is Steve? Susan's having shoulder surgery next month. He'll be in for some drama, for sure," Mom said.

"Who cares about Susan? She was a total bitch to you."

"Whoa, missy." Her eyes grew wide in a phony offended glare. "Language."

"Oh, whatever, Mom. It's true, and you don't like her. Admit it."

I respected my mother's no-nonsense attitude about manners and decorum, but it could wear on me. So many rules of polite society that she'd considered herself to be a part of, like some Southern Antebellum duchess.

She was born in Virginia, and maybe two centuries ago, her family was known as southern royalty, but this was California in the twenty-first century. I fucking couldn't care less.

"I told him to draw up the bankruptcy papers. Only Dad can sign them. I'm not a stakeholder." She wasn't either, not since she'd signed over her stakes in the divorce to avoid paying my father half of her assets or alimony. "But I don't know where he is."

Dad sometimes told Brad where he went, but not me, and certainly not Mom.

I leaned back, kicked off my Gucci sneakers, and put my feet up on the ottoman/coffee table. I jarred the wood tray holding several remote controls and an Alexa device.

Mom ignored my clumsiness, continuing her diatribe. "Did he *really* use Bernadette Spiro for his realtor?" It wasn't a question but more of a statement and a snippy one. "Alexa, play Louis Armstrong."

A soft jazzy trumpet came from hidden speakers.

"Mom, I don't know and don't care." I glared at her. "I have to find him."

She shrugged with indifference.

I dropped my head into my hands and relented to being on my own.

"Honey, I'm worried about your mental health. Your aura's all red. Why don't you go see Ramanda?"

I groaned.

About ten years ago, Mom and her friends consulted a spiritual advisor, and they still swear by her stupid tarot cards and ridiculous crystals. I'd gone once, and once was enough. She'd pissed me off when she told me my womb wouldn't work, especially not the way my husband expected it to.

I think about that all the time.

Looking back at what she'd said, maybe she had a point. David blamed me like I wasn't concentrating enough, that I drank too much Diet Coke, and that my adolescent bout with bulimia (a short-lived peer-pressure thing I'd only done twice) had to do with my inability to produce an heir for his kingdom.

I love Mom; she's my hero with her designs and standing up to Dad and even Grandpa whenever he mentioned that Dad was a lazy white trash surfer who had no idea how to run a business. Both men had epic misogynistic views of Mom's role in business and life. She hadn't stopped pushing back and had gotten her way even if the road there was messy.

As she petted her cat and sipped her tea, her degree of caring about Tennent Surf Company was at a harmfully low level. She wouldn't help, as I'd expected.

~ * ~

At about one in the afternoon, I left Mom half-asleep on her lounger chair and drove, top down with Limp Bizkit on repeat blasting, to our small warehouse. We'd downsized from our facility in Tustin, which had been Tennent's home for thirty years. Now we had a split room garage, one side design room and the other storage, two offices, and a bathroom.

When I turned into the one parking spot between ours and the industrial space next door, the metal door was rolled up.

Our employees were down to three—Tina, who'd been Dad's assistant since the 1980s; Javier, the warehouse/shipping manager, had thirty underlings at one point, but now it was just him. Last was Dottie, Mom's pattern maker, who'd forgone a paycheck for over a year. She simply intended to be helpful.

Since Walmart ordered just the two pieces in different colors every season, she had little to do. She'd putter around and organize things. She was a sweet woman, and we gave her things to keep her busy.

A smirking Brad was in his office staring at his iPhone. I smothered the urge to smack his face for the unfortunate existence of being a man in my vicinity. He glanced through the glass partition separating his office from the warehouse space.

I scowled at him, and I might have growled.

Brad, my older brother by two years, would rather be anywhere except working. For the past sixteen years, we had one customer. He'd served no purpose as sales manager.

"I'm putting you on straight commission from now on," I barked when he followed me into Dad's former office that I'd commandeered in my mutiny to keep our shipwreck from sinking. An image of the Kraken from *Clash of the Titans* popped into my head.

*Ooooh… Greek Titans on surfboards would be cool T-shirts—Medusa, Minotaur, and The Kraken. I'll have to revisit that idea.*

Sauntering in behind me, Brad whistled some unrecognizable tune with his stunning tanned skin and floppy blond hair. He was a pretty boy, and he knew it. After Jason retired, Mom convinced Brad to be our model, and he'd become quite popular.

Walmart had control over advertising creatives, and we had no say in their choice of models after that. Also, we couldn't sponsor any more surfers—a dark period in the life of Tennent Surf.

"Walmart dropped us." I exhaled and fell into the desk chair that was much too big for me. It was made for a prominent man—all leather and musk-scented.

"I knew it," he said and sat in the leather director's chair in front of the desk, kicking his feet up on it.

That made me boil over my already scorching pot. He couldn't possibly have known before me. He was being pessimistic, which was unusual for him. While I was dark and broody, my brother was a light and positive being—the ying to my yang.

"If you knew, you could've saved me from having to see Uncle Steve."

Brad slid his feet from the desk and sat up, pin-straight. "W-what did he say? Does he know where Dad is?"

Oh, Brad. My poor brother had Dad on a pedestal so tall the man could touch God.

I shook my head. "He would've told me if he did." *At least, I hoped he would.* "Dad has to sign the company over to us. Then we can start bankruptcy."

"Which one, the 'sale of the assets—one' or the 'restructuring—one?'"

"Whatever gets us out of this mess." I opened my laptop to three email notifications on my business account. All spam.

Tina appeared in my doorway. The late-middle-aged woman

with big curly hair and bright red lipstick hovered and tapped her long fake nails on the door frame.

"Hi. What's up?" I asked.

She giggled. Her cheeks were flushed pink. "Jason Mattis is on the phone asking for Gus. I told him he wasn't here, but you were, and he's on hold to talk to you."

This time, I straightened. Jason Mattis was a three-time World Surf Champion, a legend. "The Zen Shredder" was what Dad had called him and eventually, the whole world had too.

"Let's dance," Brad sang with a big smile. "Wow."

"Oh…my." I huffed like a thirteen-year-old girl whose first crush called her.

"Line one," Tina said, then returned to her desk.

I smoothed my hair as if he could see me.

Brad scoffed. "Just answer it."

I picked up the receiver and pressed line one. "Jason Mattis, as I live and breathe." I sounded like Mom with her southern belle accent. I winced.

"Rainbow Dash, how are you, My Little Pony-girl?"

The mention of his nickname for me when I was eight years old and carried around a "My Little Pony 'Rainbow Dash' doll everywhere, even to the beach, broke me.

I put my hand to my mouth and shut my eyes as the tears pierced my flimsy armor. I took a shaky breath, and it just flowed. The dam burst, followed by loud and raw sobs from the long-restrained strength I tried to portray. I covered the wails from behind my hand.

Brad grabbed the receiver, and Tina rushed to me with a box of tissues. The humiliation would start soon, but I had to let it out. It was all too much.

# Chapter Two

*Capistrano Beach, California*
*Ben*

"Count to ten," Jason told me as we bobbed on our boards in the too-early morning. The sun was at our backs and starting to burn the tips of my ears.

My soon-to-be brother-in-law made me promise to surf with him on his mission to help me "launder my karma." Which was bullshit *and* interesting. When he'd offered to give me the money I'd owed Marisol's father after he fired me and she kicked me out, I agreed to do whatever Jason told me to. If karma was a thing, then, yeah, mine was a bit dirty.

I inhaled and held it. "One, two, three, four, five—" I spat out the numbers, not understanding "The Zen Shredder's" assignment.

"No, man. Slower."

I exhaled and peered at the legend, the world surf champion, hero of every kid from Huntington Beach, striving to be more than a lower-middle class, boring, structured human.

Jason was the fantasy of what the son of a truck driver could do. He'd married a supermodel once upon a time and owned a private jet company. Now he was back in California with my sister, and they were getting married. My old, chubby, OCD, hospital corners, excel spreadsheet-loving sister was marrying the coolest dude on the planet.

"Can I do it later?" I whined like a toddler.

Waves lapped against my legs and swept onto the surfboard. Usually, the water was a calm space, but with Jason Mattis–yep, that Jason Mattis—right beside me telling me to take things slow, it wasn't so relaxing.

"Why?" he asked. "You have someplace to be?"

*No, I didn't.* "I-I'll do it when I get mad," I told him.

"That's fair but slower. Don't do anything until you count."

My anger issues had gotten me into hot water most of my life, including being arrested twice and jailed when I was eighteen. Jason was the first person to make me face the rage in a way I was open to. I respected him, and I was getting too old for that kind of shit.

I raked a hand through my hair. It was too early for most people to be out, but carrying our boards into the surf, Jason and I turned the heads of a few female joggers. The Zen Shredder was twelve years older than me and looked damn good. I liked to think I still had it too. At forty-one, I did daily weight training. Not bad for a couple of middle-aged guys.

So, yeah, maybe I didn't *appear* all that old. Everything in me was wrung out, tired, and sick of battling the fury inside me. "But what if I can't get to ten every single time something pisses me off?"

It wasn't a question but an attempt to be a sarcastic jerk because I got pissed off a lot.

Jason splashed me, and the water cooled my burning skin. It was crazy hot weather in December, in the high eighties. *Fucking global warming.*

"Okay," he said, " so since there are no waves, go home. I'll get you around eleven."

I sighed. That was an order because that was what Jason did. Order me around. I was his pussy-boy because he'd bailed me out and forced me to be his 'assistant' like in a sappy TV sit-com, running his errands, scraping surfboards until the chemicals burned my eyes, then hanging supports and organizing the boards in his garage. I was laundering my karma with slave labor and humility.

Better than owing Marisol's family anything.

Still, as I sprawled on my belly to start the paddle to shore, I wondered where I'd be when I was Jason's age. Married? A good job that I liked?

"What happens at eleven?" I asked.

"We're going to see the Tennents, your new employer." Jason raised his gaze to the north, then back at me. *Still no waves.*

"Tennent Surf?" I asked.

"Yeah, Lisa's in charge. There's been some stuff going down. I think I can help them. I owe it to her. Her old man always believed in me," Jason said.

"Their shit is only in Walmart. You know that, right? They don't make boards anymore."

"Then it's worse than I thought." Jason sighed.

The surfing legend had been living in Brazil for the past twenty years and had missed the publicly humiliating death of his old sponsor's rein of coolness.

We started the grueling paddle back, and even with weight training every day, the burn could kill my old ass.

~ * ~

Jason steered his white pickup truck into a run-down industrial park next to the South Coast Plaza Mall, one of my teenage hangouts in the 1990s, which now was an old, outdated memory of another time.

"I can't believe Tennent Surf is in this place," I mused. Tennent Surf was the iconic brand of my teen years. A new T-shirt was released every year with the sickest graphics, and my red 'TSC' hat was my signature. "I thought they'd have some big complex out east."

"They used to." He was as disappointed as I was about the fall of the epic brand. "This is devastating."

We drove past a line of metal garage-door buildings, one after the other until we got to a cheap vinyl banner over the garage door.

*Tennent Surf Co.*

Held up by zip ties.

What a fall from grace.

The glass side door burst open as we approached, causing that cheap banner to fly. A weeping older woman rushed to Jason and threw her arms around him. She had wadded tissues in her hand and rocked him side-to-side like he was a POW home from war. When they stepped apart, they wore big smiles, and Jason seemed like he could cry too.

"The prodigal son has returned," she said.

I passed them into the building and ventured down a putty-colored hallway with my curiosity at a dangerous level. I slinked away from the reunion as another lady, this one older than the first, hugged The Zen Shredder.

"Motherfucking son of a fucking bitch. Of all the stupid damn shit. Fuck. Fuck. Fucking. F-f-f..." a woman shouted like she had a Ph.D. in swear words.

I approached a shaking metal storage cabinet with the door swinging. It flew open to reveal a stunning tight ass in a pair of skinny jeans.

"Wow," I said to the jeans, wiping my thumb and pointer fingers down the corners of my mouth in case I'd drooled.

Thick blonde locks flew upward and back to reveal the biggest brown eyes.

She ignored me after making eye contact, but I'd never be the same. Some invisible fist sucker-punched me in the gut, and I had to step back, clutching my midsection.

*Must help the damsel in distress.*

"How about some help?" A deep masculine voice came from me. Why did I lower my voice? I'm not an overcompensating twelve-year-old soprano.

"Not from you." Her top half disappeared into the cabinet again. This time, she forced a nylon bag out and stumbled a few steps before righting herself. Then she marched away, huffing and puffing.

I followed her—probably a bad idea.

Highlighted blonde hair hit just below the shoulders in that South-County-rich-women-with-a-mansion-on-the-hill style. The hair of a woman with two spoiled kids and a husband who had a master's degree and wore a suit to the office. Her AG jeans were cropped and flared at the ankle, and her Gucci stripe sneakers had black scuffs on the back.

Yup, she was the epitome of an Orange County housewife. Except, I hadn't heard that language from any of those women, except for other OC housewives.

She was about my age and smoking hot.

Entering an office, she flung the bag on the desk with a thud and finally noticed me at the door. "Who are you?"

"Oh." I jumped, launched forward, then stopped and debated whether to shake her hand like a proper subordinate to a superior or shove my hands into my pockets like the arrogant prick I was. I chose the latter. "I'm Ben Stringer, Jason's assistant."

I was overcome by a wave of heat hitting my body. She radiated power and anger, and I was drawn to it like a car crash.

"Assistant?" she scoffed. "That's perfect."

The comment hit but didn't sink in. "Perfect, yeah. Why exactly?"

I knew what she was all about—rich and spoiled from Newport or Laguna, mean girl, and way out of my league. Still, she was so fucking hot.

She waved her hand up and down at me. "Because—"

I peered down and examined what I was wearing: a backward hat, a Von Dutch T-shirt, plaid shorts, and my blue on-blue 'Old Skool' Vans.

"Hey, Lisa." Jason came up behind me.

She pushed past me and threw her arms around Jason's shoulders. They hugged for longer than I was comfortable with. "You're here. You're really here." Her eyes welled up. They stepped back and regarded each other.

"In the flesh," he joked and threw his arm over her shoulder, bumping me on purpose as they moved farther into the office.

She motioned for him to sit in the chair opposite the desk while she circled it and settled in an oversized leather chair, like the boss.

I sank onto a mini couch big enough for one person or maybe two little kids.

"I was hoping to talk in private. It's all kind of sensitive." She glared at me.

Jason leaned forward with his elbows on his knees. "How much, Lisa? Give me the whole number."

Like a cat in the dark, her eyes widened, and her mouth dropped open. She seemed like the kind of woman who wasn't surprised by much, and this expression was so candid I almost felt like I was intruding.

"I-I wasn't prepared for that question. I'd have to do a prospectus—and get my P & L's—a-and—" She turned to her laptop and fired it up.

"Okay, that's fine." Jason straightened. "Now for the personal stuff." He turned to me. "Ben, can you excuse us for a minute?"

I chuckled at his voice which was so chill compared to her frantic stuttering.

This woman had issues, maybe more than me. Her anxiety charged the air like electric currents, shocking anyone who could get close to her. To me, it was like an incredible glow, all blue and sparking. I imagined she'd make crackling noises in her sleep.

I shoved my hands into my pockets and left the office. Passing the cabinet she was fighting with, I was about to close the door when I saw printouts of graphics: cheesy sunsets, surfers, and tropical beaches. I rolled my eyes. They must've been graphics for the Walmart T-shirts.

I yanked them out and studied them. They were computer-generated crap and not worthy of the legendary company's name. Yeah. Damn, fall from grace, for sure.

"Hey, what are you doing?" The older-older woman tried to shout at me but ended up coughing into a handkerchief.

She stopped her fit long enough to ask, "Are you the new model? You look like a model."

I let out a guffaw. "Me? A model? *Surely* you must be joking."

"A fit model, hottie, and don't call me *Shirley*."

My jaw dropped as Lisa's did. The old woman had just quoted the movie *Airplane* and called me 'hottie.'"

"Uh, okay." That was all I could say without busting out laughing. "I won't call you Shirley."

"I couldn't give a fuck; it happens to be my name," she quipped with a grin.

*Wait. Seriously?*

Then she leaned forward, let out a wheezy laugh, and held her midsection. "Oh, man, did I get you good, slick."

I huffed an obligatory laugh, the kind when someone tells an awful dad joke. "Yeah, you sure did."

She sighed and eyed me from head to toe. "Name's Dottie. Come here, stud. I need a fit model, and you've got some nice shoulders." She waved toward the hallway and started walking.

I followed her, shaking my head. *What a character.* "I'm Ben, Jason's assistant."

She wheezed through another laugh, then coughed again. "Assistant?" she rasped. "What in the hell kind of job is that? Why would an old surfer have a fucking assistant?"

"Um, well, I owe him, so I'm gonna assist him until I work off my debt." I cringed at the honest confession of being a 'pussy-boy.'

"Jason's a clever man." She smiled and stopped at a long green table with a graph pattern etched into it like from high school math.

It also had old-fashioned wooden rulers glued to the edges with inches and feet highlighted. Strangely shaped parchment paper resembling dismembered limbs laid on top.

She picked one up and held it to my arm at the shoulder to my wrist. It was the exact length to my watch band. She nodded, took another, longer one, and held it to my hip. Again, another perfect fit.

"Yup, you're perfect, handsome."

"For what?" I chuckled at the 'handsome' endearment.

She turned toward a rolling rack behind her and handed me a long-sleeved T-shirt and a pair of plaid shorts.

"Let's see those tatts, you bad boy. Do you have them everywhere?" Her eyebrows wiggled as she scanned the colorful images—my life story—covering my upper body. "Strip."

"What?"

"Oh, for heaven's sake, *priss*. Go in the bathroom and put these on if you're going to be like that."

Did she call me a 'priss?' As in 'prissy?' Or 'prude?'

"Okay, but only for you, beautiful," I clapped back, and her smile lit me up.

I stepped into the changing room while trying to get my head straight—my focus on the here and now. I was at Tennent Surf, a company I'd worshipped as a teen.

Dottie made me think of my grandmother, Eileen. I pictured my sweet mother. It got harder for me to visit home lately, and I missed my mother's selfless, non-judgmental hugs. Being at Tennent reminded me of the days when Grandma Eileen was still around, and Dad wasn't ill with Alzheimer's.

He could barely remember me anymore. When he did recognize me, he warned me not to break anything or pitch a fit, like I was four years old. The discomfort of being around him was the main reason I hadn't visited in quite a while.

The fabric was soft as it slid on my body. I closed my eyes, pinched the bridge of my nose, and breathed deeply.

Dad and I had a complicated relationship because I'd been the 'problem child.' I was terrible at school and chose to draw and daydream. When anyone told me to focus, I'd get angry, sometimes violent. I liked to break things and get into fights. Dad didn't think art was appropriate for a real man.

I'd even tried to appease us both by attempting to study architecture, in the same world as his commercial elevator sales career. The classes were boring, and too much damn math. No matter what, somehow, the topic of school always ended in an argument.

*Breathe, Ben. Breathe. Count to ten.*

Drowning in the clothes, I came out of the bathroom. I held my arms out, but the shorts fell to my ankles. We laughed.

"Great legs, Ben." Dottie giggled.

I tugged the shorts up, and she came at me with a plush tomato wrapped around her bony wrist. She turned into white lightning, pinning the seams to fit loosely but tighter than before.

"Okay, get out of those, and mind the pins."

I went back and carefully removed the garments, euphoric that I'd helped someone.

Even though I had significant anger issues, I loved the idea of being a hero. I was more like Batman, all growly and anti-social. Only a few people in my life knew I had that personality quirk. Except Bruce Wayne was a rich dude and could get away with an alter ego. With a police record and tattoos, I was just the ex-convict son of an elevator salesman. I still had the calling to do the right thing.

When I returned, Lisa and Jason leaned over drawings on the green table.

I handed the clothes to Dottie, and she left the room.

"Hey, you met Miss Dottie, huh?" Jason asked as I sidled to the other side of the large table to get a good view of Lisa.

"Yeah, she's—"

They chuckled.

Lisa glanced up at me, and I swear she sent a spark to my arms.

I don't think I've ever had goosebumps before, but the prickly feeling had been described to me, and now I was covered in them.

I wondered if she tasted like Sweetarts candies, not honey or anything syrupy, but. drooling, addicting, sugary—sour. My mouth filled with saliva.

*What are these things happening to me just being in her vicinity?*

"After we talked yesterday, I got my shit together and drew these—" Lisa passed the sketches to Jason. "The Surf-Skate-Snow Show is in San Diego in one month, and I hope to have samples by then."

"Endless Summer by Jason Mattis?" I picked up a graphic with the silhouette of a surfer on a yellow and orange background, like the famous movie poster.

She didn't acknowledge me.

"What do you mean '*by* Jason Mattis'?" Jason peered at her.

She stepped back, and her face changed from pride to fear.

"I-if it's with your name, we might gain some respect." She frowned and glanced at her sketches. "We've got to get back to being cool. The last sixteen years destroyed our reputation."

He spread the sketches out, leaned forward with his elbows on the table peering down at them, then up at me. "What do you think, Ben?"

Lisa stared at me. Her soft brown eyes melted my insides.

"Yeah, I think it might work," I blurted out.

It was a brilliant plan. Damn, she was gorgeous and smart too. Forget out of my league. She was out of my universe.

"You don't have to do anything, Jason." Her excitement peaked. "I'll do it all and run it past you for approval."

He nodded. "Okay, let's do it, but no big straw hat like your pop used to wear. He looked like a kook."

She laughed, and her breathing picked up. Shaking in her exhale, her smile fell. Her chest heaved like she couldn't get enough air. I knew that feeling all too well. It was the beginning of an anxiety attack.

"Breathe, Lisa. I'm all in. You're my family. We will right this ship, I promise." Jason took her by the shoulders.

She fell against his chest and threw her arms around him again. "I'll make sure you are cool as shit, 'Zen Shredder.' I promise."

My body warmed at that. He was going to save her and the Tennent brand. I wanted to save her, too, if she'd let me.

# Chapter Three

*Lisa*

I'd found several old samples of the last line we'd done with Jason in 1999 and was blown away by how Mom constructed the pieces to all go together with fabrics and color schemes. Every piece coordinated with the other. She was the master, and I would follow her lead but with updates.

Jason's assistant's throwback skater-punk look inspired me, and I couldn't get him out of my head. It was ridiculous; the man was *not* my type. I'd never dated anyone with tattoos and never wanted to. I was itching to see all of his, or maybe just him with his shirt off.

*Oh, shit, I'm having a breakdown/mid-life crisis.*

"He's got great legs, that Ben-cutie," Dottie said, peering over the glasses on the bridge of her nose from the sewing machine across the room. "Haven't seen legs like that in years. Even better than Jason's."

"You think he's sexy?" I asked.

"Don't you?"

Yes, I did in the wrong-side-of-the-tracks-bad-boy sort of way. I'm too old for that shit. He also seemed like trouble, like he'd bring too much drama. Not what I could handle in my current dumpster fire life.

"Nope," I lied.

"Uh-huh." She knew I was full of shit. She always did.

I took a breath, about to go back to the drawings, when a voice filled the room. It was deep, masculine, and attractive as hell. It tightened my stomach and tingled my lady parts.

My whole body seized up. *Ben.* Here to get swatches for Jason. Dottie cackled as if she'd conjured him like the witch I'd suspected her to be.

Ben's cool demeanor changed to giddy when he noticed something beside me. He hurried over to the rolling rack and took the jacket off.

"No way. I wanted this jacket so bad when I was—" He stopped before he revealed his age.

The plaid, flannel jacket with a satin quilt lining was the signature piece from the 1995 line. It'd sold out multiple times, and we kept it on rotation with different patterns until…Walmart.

"How come you didn't buy it?" I asked.

He slipped his arms in, flipped it onto his broad shoulders, and went to the full-length mirror next to Dottie, who stood and admired him. "I couldn't afford it. It was like eighty bucks. I didn't have that much for a jacket back then."

How many of the local boys couldn't afford the jacket? Tennent was supposed to make clothes for surfers and skaters using the local trends from those boys, then we priced them out.

"You know what would be epic?" He raised his arm in the air. "Some grommeted vent holes. Yeah, it gets hot, but I'd wear this beauty all year round, especially after getting out of the water. Some vent holes hidden under the arms would be cool."

Wow. I don't know what I thought Ben would say about the jacket, maybe that it was a nice color, but not this. Grommets and vent holes? The guys I dealt with didn't know anything about that sort of stuff.

He must've noticed my shock because he added, "If you can do it. I mean, it's not a big deal."

Dottie grinned at me, her drawn on eyebrows sky high.

"We could do that," I snapped and started my pattern cutting.

"Well, I'll get out of your hair. I'll just take the swatches." He took off the jacket and carefully placed it on the rack.

I glimpsed his tight abs before he pulled down the hem of his T-shirt. He caught me ogling him. *Shit.*

"Uh, they're over here." I collected the scraps of cotton jersey, flannel, and poplin in different patterns and thicknesses.

He was beside me in a flash, wearing an enormous, wicked grin. Even though he was rough everywhere else, his smile was like my most sinful, wettest dream. A vision of him hovering over me, shirtless with that naughty expression on his face, like he knew something I didn't, made my Kegel muscles clench and pulse.

"Not that one." He put an orange and green plaid scrap aside. "Or this." He flung a polka-dotted swatch across the table in mock disgust.

Bold action but impressive.

I nodded. They were not to my taste either.

He was leaning into me, smelling of citrus and fresh air, and I thought about him staying there until I could have his scent all over me. If I inhaled him any longer, I'd most likely get addicted to it. That was what he was, a drug—a quick fix of euphoria. *Nope, nope, nope.*

"Can you back up a little?" I glared at him.

"Why?" he breathed out, gazing hungrily at my chest then my lips while rubbing his together.

His proximity was heating me like I was being burned at the stake for what I imagined him doing to me—all biting and pounding and orgasms: *pulse, clench, pulse, clench.*

I might be shaking. Man, I was all kinds of messed up.

I finally pushed him, and he stepped back, his strong brow furrowing in confusion.

"I'm setting some ground rules here," I said with authority.

"Whatever you say, boss."

I flinched at 'boss.' *Am I really the boss?* Dottie's sewing machine whirred, and she couldn't hear what I was about to say to my relief since she liked him.

"Look, you're not my type, okay. What are you stuck in the '90s? With your 909'er-Fred Durst-Skater douchey—baggy short, flat cap, and cheesy-ass chain wallet. Oh, I know, it's a Peter Pan complex. That's it. You're not what I need or want right now."

He extracted the wallet from his pocket and held it up to show me. "Excuse me. This is Alexander McQueen. Only one hundred were produced. Italian leather and stainless-steel studs."

"Probably a fake," I snarked.

He closed the distance between us and peered at me from his six-foot frame; his scent wafted up my nose, making me imagine licking his neck. "Resale, but *not* fake," he growled.

If he wrapped his arms around me and grabbed my ass, drew me to his heat-radiating body, pressing our sex together, maybe the ache would go away.

But he didn't. He picked up the fabric pieces and turned away. "See you Sunday," he growled again.

Totally pussy clenching sexy? *Shit, I have issues.* "Sunday?"

"Jason's wedding. You and Brad are coming. My sister told me they'd invited you."

*Damnit, I'd forgotten.* "Yes, of course. We'll be there." *Got to get a gift. Just another fucking thing to stress about.*

"Bye, Dottie-hottie," he sang sweetly to my pattern maker.

She blew him a kiss and continued sewing.

He peered over his shoulder and shook his head at me like I'd made a colossal mistake poking his growly bear. Why was that sexy too? I rolled my eyes at myself.

"I need therapy," I murmured to nobody.

"Or to get laid," the witch called from across the room.

*Creepy old lady.*

# Chapter Four

*Ben*

"Now, get out, so I can be alone with my wife," Jason shouted from the stucco half wall on the patio, ducking string lights.

My sister's house sat right on Capistrano Beach, far south of where we grew up and rich as hell. The cement patio surrounding a half wall separated it from the sand, and a bonfire raged on the beach several feet away, making everything glow.

Shelly's house was the perfect place for her wedding to the surf legend. After their simple sunset ceremony, we'd gathered on her beachfront patio for a champagne toast. The sun had set into the ocean, and a peach sky reflected in the patio's sliding glass doors.

"That's your speech?" Brad Tennent teased.

Jason jumped down, grabbed my sister, and kissed her.

Brad turned to me. "I guess that's his speech." He shrugged. This guy was kind of a dim-pretty boy that I had little patience for.

"A man of few words." I shrugged back.

The small gathering was mainly family—my parents and nephews, Jason's dad and new wife, Jason's daughter, Jasmine, and the Tennents.

Lisa wore a light green embossed dress celebrating her curves and strong legs. The skirt hit mid-thigh in the front, but when it accommodated her luscious round ass, the skirt rode up a little in the back. Not that I was complaining.

She held a champagne glass, giggled with my sister and Jasmine, then glanced at me.

I gave her space but watched as she downed the entire glass.

Shelly filled it, and Lisa swallowed it again. Her big brown eyes were fixed on me.

What was this?

I'd been obsessing over her for weeks. I was having too many filthy dreams and masturbation fodder starring her. After seeing her at the warehouse Thursday night, I knew something was between us even though she'd made up that stuff about 'ground rules' and called me a '909'er.'

She'd leaned over that table, showing her cleavage on purpose, but then retreated. She was going through a lot with the business failing and her father disappearing. I'd be stressed too, but I wouldn't ignore the obvious attraction we had. She was playing a game where the rules changed to suit her mood, and I was already losing.

I'd almost drunk a bottle of tequila while my thumb hovered over her number for hours that night, finally passing out on my grandmother's velvet, tufted settee.

I'd taken over Grandma Eileen's lease with rent control at an old East Huntington apartment building. She'd been there for over thirty years, and it was cheap and clean, but when she passed away earlier in the year, her lease was still something my parents paid for.

I'd moved in after Marisol threw my stuff into the carpark from the bedroom window of the apartment we'd shared for three years. I'd been a monk ever since, feeling like I wasn't worthy of anyone's attention or sympathy.

Jason changed that. He believed in me for some god-forsaken reason. I wasn't going to let him down. I resonated with his energy to help people without asking for anything in return. I wanted to help her.

When Lisa sauntered toward me, my inner Batman sprung to life. *Be cool, Ben. Like Bruce Wayne, play it cool.*

Jason threw his arm around her shoulder, then led her the rest of the way to me, throwing the other arm around me so we all faced my sister. He hadn't stopped smiling the entire time, and it was infectious.

"I just married the girl who almost got away from me forever. You just don't fucking know." He dropped his arms, then opened the cooler and took a beer. "But fuck luck, you know. I went and got her. Made damn sure she couldn't get away this time." He tipped his beer to us, then walked over to Shelly and his daughter Jasmine.

When Shelly's husband, Eric, died, she'd written a book like the overachiever she was. It wasn't about her tragic life. It was a cheesy romance novel loosely based on her affair with Jason in their twenties. The book became an international bestseller.

A few months ago, Jason, who was divorced, left Brazil to find her at a book signing in Vancouver. Now they're married. The Zen Shredder married my sister, and I'm his assistant. Life's crazy like that.

I glanced at Lisa; her face was pure lust and intentions.

"What's up, boss?" I took a swig and avoided her gaze. She was drunk and not right in the head space.

"Refill." She dangled her glass.

Jason and Shelly started dirty dancing, rubbing against each other, then he dipped her back, kissing her neck. They were like teenagers instead of fifty-year-old parents of grown humans.

I whooped, and Brad hooted from across the patio.

Mom huffed her disapproval before storming inside through the sliding glass door. I giggled at that. Mom was a product of the Victorian era with her handkerchiefs and teapots. Puritan to the core.

My nephews groaned and turned away, embarrassed. Their pimply, teenage asses wished they had girls to dance with like that.

I opened the cooler, took out an open bottle of champagne, and filled Lisa's glass. She downed it again. That was three I'd witnessed.

"Are you worried about prohibition coming back?" I said to her.

She shook the glass, and I filled it again.

"Weddings make me drink," she croaked.

I wanted to stare at her for the rest of the night, taking in every feature. The color of the peach sunset glowed high on her cheeks, and her eyes were luminous. Beneath that beauty, there was something sad about her. Fresh air and some distance from happy, dancing couples was my prescription.

"Let's take a walk." I took the bottle and strolled out the small gate onto the sand.

My nephews had built a bonfire, sending waves of heat to my face, and as Lisa kicked off her heels and moseyed to me, I became breathless.

She grinned, but the energy coming from her wasn't happy.

"Oh, good, you brought the bottle." She passed me with exaggerated swaying hips and swished toward the dark shore.

I gave her more space to see what she'd do while enjoying the view from behind too much.

She stopped at the water's edge, turned to me, then to the ocean. Then she laid onto the sand, her knees bent and swaying from side-to-side. When I caught up to her, she was singing. Nickelback's "How You Remind Me." A song I knew all too well. She stopped when I stood over her.

"Are we having fun yet?" I asked, cocking my head.

She giggled, and her cleavage jiggled. Damnit, if I could bury myself in her breasts…

She reached for my hand, then yanked me down beside her, but I didn't lie down. I just stared at her legs.

It was an unusually warm day in December, but the cool western breeze was picking up from the frigid Pacific.

"I'm not having fun. At all." She sat up and took the champagne bottle, chugging right from it. "My father is a piece of shit. My ex is a bigger piece of shit. My brother is a lazy fuck, and my Uncle Steve thinks I'm perpetually eight years old. All men are useless."

I took the bottle and swigged it too. "Yup, and we're getting more and more obsolete."

Her eyes opened wider at that comment. "Yes, I don't need any of you." She grabbed the bottle. "Fuck all of you. Except for Jason. He can stay, but he's married."

"You like Jason?"

"No, he's too old for me," she scoffed. "The idea of him, you know? He helps people." She turned toward me. "He's going to start a surf school for underprivileged and physically challenged kids. The man's a fucking saint."

He'd mentioned it to me. She was right. He was too good for this world, but I liked having him in it to remind me that not everyone was out to make me feel like shit. If I'd had Jason in my life years ago, I wouldn't have done eighteen months in jail for aggravated assault.

Then 'anger management' and 'rehab.' Only to go back a few years after for dealing in illegal substances, both on my permanent record for potential jobs. No one would hire me except Marisol's dad to fix motorcycles, and I was happy to take it and accept her aggressive advances too.

Fixing cars and motorcycles made sense to me. I'd been doing it since I was fourteen at my buddy's dad's gas station on the corner of my street. I'd bounced around from one garage to the next, leaving after an altercation with the boss or the other mechanics. Too much macho-testosterone-filled shit for me to contain myself.

I'd always be the loser little brother to my golden-girl sister who'd gone to law school, married another lawyer, and moved to the South County, a world away from the grease-stained streets and traffic of North County. That was my world. College seemed like too much work, and fixing things gave me purpose.

"Your sister's amazing," Lisa added. "I read her book. She loves Jason. They love each other." She stopped and put her head in her hands. Then she raised her head, took a deep breath from her nose, and let it out of her mouth. Tears sat on her cheekbones, shining in the moonlight.

My heart broke. "What happened to you? I heard Jason call you Rainbow Dash."

She put the bottle to her lips and paused, staring at the waves. "I used to be all rainbows and sunshine. I carried a Rainbow Dash doll everywhere, you know, from My Little Pony?" She faced me and sniffed in her tears.

"I have a daughter," I confessed. "But I haven't seen her in months. She likes My Little Pony."

I was unsure where I thought that information fit into our conversation except that I, unlike her, had been dark and angry most of my life until Chloe. Then a sunrise woke me up. Not even jail and rehab had turned on that light. The thought of getting married and having a child changed me. Or it could've been my age.

I was just ready. I would marry Marisol, work at her father's garage, and raise our daughter. Life would be good, simple, and stationary until Mari showed me a different side of her when we moved in together; delusional, possessive, and jealous.

Lisa started light and was now dark and stormy. I knew where she was at.

She ignored my comment about Chloe, probably assuming I was some royal fuck up. Unmarried, with a kid that I hadn't acknowledged. I'll bet she thought I cheated on her mother and had other kids I didn't see. I had no delusions about how people perceived me.

"It's getting cold. Can you give me a ride home?" She stood and brushed sand from her legs.

Something about the way she'd asked wasn't a question. It was an order: '*I require a good fuck, and you are my guy.*

"Are you sure?"

She nodded but added, "It's just a ride, though. Don't get any ideas."

"Mm-hmm. Right, you're my boss."

"No, Jason is. I'm—" She took two steps closer and tilted her head back to see my face.

I lifted my chin. I couldn't look into her eyes because I'd take her right there in the sand. Damnit, I couldn't help it. Traitors. My gaze wandered down, locking with the blue sparks crackling in her dark brown eyes. My body went hot.

She kissed my jaw. "I'm not your boss."

Her mixed signals weren't phasing me. I knew what was going on. She was going through a tough time, had a loaded gun of anger, and was lonely in her current state of hell. I could relate.

Being around her made me feel like I was the sane one for the first time in my life. For once, I was steady while someone else was having an existential crisis. Having been through that gauntlet, sex was what she wanted now. A stress reliever and escape. She was fortunate or just perceptive that one of my few talents lay in that act.

If this would help her, then I would be her hero.

# Chapter Five

*Lisa*

I'd never ridden on the back of a motorcycle. The vibration beneath me and the man between my legs turned me on and confused me. I was terrified when we were on the 73-freeway, weaving through traffic, but Ben was in control. He guided the motorcycle easily and confidently. I clung to him as if my life depended on it.

He helped me off the bike when we reached my house. The skirt of my dress was almost at my waist; I was going to yank it down, but my hands stayed on his shoulders a little too long. He stared at me like I was supposed to say something. I didn't.

I gripped his shoulders and envisioned wrapping my legs around his torso and rubbing up and down his washboard stomach. I pushed him away before he could lean in and kiss me.

My body was all in, but my head was doing a number.

*Stop sending him mixed signals.*

He chuckled and shoved his hands into his jean's pockets. I studied his outfit, a significant departure from every other time I'd seen him. He was wearing a light blue, linen Cuban guayabera-style button-down shirt. We had one in the line at one point, but this one was much nicer. Maybe another of his resale purchases.

That whole exchange about his wallet and his knowledge of designer labels surprised me from a Huntington guy, and the suggestion about the air holes in the flannel jacket was close to brilliant. His calm and refined attitude the whole evening was ice-cold sexy. Even though he was this gritty, cheesy dude from North County, I was frustratingly attracted to him.

He wouldn't survive in my world of white tablecloth cocktail hours, country club mixers, and black tie charity events. No, he was too much ink and metal and not enough khakis and golf shirts.

Tonight would be it for us. A satisfying scratch to the itch we were suffering for the sake of workplace decorum. I hadn't been with a man in two years and craved sex with a warm body, not just my 'dildo of the month' to choose from. The last time I was with a man was an obligatory anniversary episode, devoid of any passion, and with my ex-husband.

David was from the right family, school, and career. Like all my boyfriends, he fit the mold I was supposed to find. I loved him for a long time. Until I didn't. By then, we were a couple, our friends were couples, and our families had meshed to where I'd lost consciousness of which cousins, aunts, and uncles were his and which were mine. Holidays, birthdays, anniversaries, and even deaths were as married as we were after eleven years.

It was all as it should be until I left him and, in the process, left our friends, our house, and even our dry cleaner.

If any of my old friends saw me lusting after a tattooed, motorcycle-riding dude like Ben Stringer, they'd know I was losing my mind. I was, oh boy, I was.

I padded up the steps to my townhouse door, and the light flicked on. Ben's body heat behind me and his breath down my bare shoulders was warming me *and* giving me chills.

I let him in. He strode past me and into my entryway with the massive crystal chandelier that could've been hanging in some grand hotel. I imagined what he must be thinking, taking in the ostentatious light fixture.

"Nice," he said, craning his head back to take in the extravagance.

With his hands still in his pockets, he sauntered under the arched entrance to my den and kept going through to my great room like an inspector about to give me an estimate of the property's worth.

I threw my heels off to the side of the door and followed him.

He meandered to the sliding glass door to my small backyard, then over to a bookshelf and leaned into a photo.

I was embarrassed by my housekeeping. I hadn't found a cleaner yet, and there was open mail, purses, and shoes everywhere—too lazy or busy to put anything away. There were dirty dishes in the sink and on the counter, and a funky smell from something spoiled in the trash or fridge wafted in the air.

"Is this you?" He pointed to the photo he'd been studying.

I reached the side of him and winced at my fifteen-year-old self, smiling from ear to ear in a puffy white silk dress and elbow-length gloves on the steps of the Ritz Carlton Hotel. "That was cotillion when I was fifteen."

He turned to me. "What's a 'cotillion?'"

That question surprised me until I remembered he wasn't from my society. He wasn't acquainted with the outdated practice of teaching a girl how to be a proper wife by learning to conduct small talk, set a table, walk bone straight in heels, and waltz—the precursor to being what rich men expected in a wife: pretty, clean, and quiet.

*Fuck that.*

"Um, I guess it's like manners lessons. How to behave in social situations, and cotillion is the celebration of what you've learned with a—" I gulped at how antiquated it sounded. "A debutante ball."

"So, like princess lessons?" He grinned.

"No." I scowled as I walked away.

Then I thought about it for a moment. The traditional root of the exercise had been to ready ladies for a 'coming out' where she'd be on display for eligible and vetted men for marriage.

I sighed. "Yeah, I guess it kind of was."

"Weird. Like you were some prized racehorse that would be put with a stud to make more prized racehorses."

"Except I can't make racehorses or any other kind of babies." I opened my wine fridge. "I'm going to have more to drink. How about you?"

I appreciated that he didn't ask me to elaborate about not having babies.

"Sure," he said as he wandered to my sizeable sectional sofa and sat. "So, what do we do now? Dishes?" His chin tipped toward my disaster of a kitchen.

"Be my guest." I searched for my champagne flutes, not remembering where I'd put them.

He didn't move from his spot on the couch.

"You seemed happy in that photo." He took the glass I handed him, which was a cordial and not a champagne flute, another lesson from the cotillion on table settings.

I sat next to him. "I was. I loved my dress, and I was super excited to show off my dancing skills."

I glanced at the photo. A deep melancholy set in. That was the night I'd gotten to wear what I'd designed for the first time, and even though my dress was more traditional, floor length with underskirts, I'd loved it, and I *was* a princess in it. A magical princess who made her beautiful gown.

But, of course, my fairytale ended. Those damn stories don't tell what happens after the 'happily ever after.' After years of trying, Cinderella was bullied into taking hormones that made her crazy and sent her mental health into a tailspin, all to produce an heir for the prince.

"I could see why Jason called you Rainbow Dash. That smile was sunshine and rainbows for sure." Ben's voice was soft and thoughtful.

His words should have consoled me; instead, they confused me. He was being suave and sophisticated even though his neck ink reminded me of his gritty persona.

If he'd been born to a South County family, he would've been one of the most sought-after guys for his handsome face alone—toned cheekbones, hazel eyes, thick dark blond hair. He was gorgeous underneath the paint and tough-guy attitude.

"Yeah, well, I'm not feeling so sunshiny and rainbows right now," I confessed, and my shoulders slumped when I recalled my shortcomings.

He gave me a gentle smile. "I think you just forgot how to fly."

His words rolled through me, and… *Shit. Do not cry, Lisa.* I must stay in control.

He was right. I had forgotten how to fly. I had forgotten how to be happy. How little things made me feel special, like dying my shoes light blue to match my big hair bow. Like floating on the dance floor with Scott Piper as we showed off how well we'd done in the dance class portion of our training and how he told me I was pretty.

"Ben, remind me how to fly." I'd been feeling sorry for myself for too long. I'd let others measure my worth, then I'd get angry about it instead of taking what I wanted.

I lifted my leg over his lap, straddling him, then took our glasses and set them behind me on the coffee table.

He put his big hands on either side of my hips and licked his lips. The skirt of my dress was up to my waist, and I adjusted right over the bulge of his jeans.

His expression was all resolved. He hungered for more of me but didn't move. He let me take control, and I couldn't have been more thankful.

"Take what you need, Lisa." His low growly voice was back and made my panties wet.

I kissed him, and when I drew away, his face hadn't changed, but his eyes had gone from light brown with flecks of gold to black.

I huffed and kissed him harder, unbuttoning his shirt quickly and tearing the fabric apart to get to his hard, colorfully painted chest. I closed my eyes, shutting out the story of his life printed on his body in permanent ink. It wasn't the time to know his life story.

I knew some of his story. The rest? That artwork would have to wait. I longed to kiss and lick every toned muscle on his chest. His breathing increased when I ran my tongue over his right nipple and nibbled lightly.

He put his hand on the back of my head, and I threw it off. He needed to understand what I craved. Surrender. He placed his arms along the back of the couch.

*Good boy.*

I raised my gaze to him, and his breath hitched when I unbuckled his heavy leather belt: another quality accessory, soft buckskin leather with a hearty stainless steel "D & G" buckle.

He grabbed the top of the couch pillows when I flicked open the button and unzipped the fly, but he didn't move. A low growl came from him when I lowered my hand down the waistband of his briefs, palmed his hardness between the flat of his stomach, and ground my hips forward to rub the other side.

"Condom," he whispered.

I glanced up from the salacious sight of the tip of his erection peeking through the top of his underwear. "I can't get pregnant and haven't been with anyone in two years."

"I was with my ex for three years and haven't been with anyone without a condom." He squeezed my ass.

I nodded, not that I could stop at this point to try and find a damn condom or make him go to the store two miles away. I was past any further discussion. This was happening now.

I tugged his waistband down and my soaked G-string to the side, guiding his hardness into me. It took me a few times lifting and lowering to accommodate his size and my neglected pussy to stretch. It was so good to be filled that way.

He unzipped my dress, lifted it over my head, and threw it to the side. When he gripped my ass and squeezed, electric currents shot to my inner muscles.

"Take it, princess," he whispered in my ear.

I rolled my hips in a clockwise scoop, hitting my clit with each meeting of his pelvic bone. He lifted his hips, swirling in the opposite direction. Each time our bodies met in the middle, the pressure got harder on me and inside me—warmth spreading from my thighs to my sex, over and over. Our rhythm was perfection, like a waltz, both partners working for my bliss.

"I'll give you anything to make you fly," he said.

The dual assault on my hotspots was buzzing power lines and a rushing river colliding with an explosion of epic proportions. My muscles tensed, and I dug my nails into his shoulders.

"Oh. Fuck," I shouted.

He pulsed his hips into me when I couldn't move anymore. I was stretched like a slingshot. I let go, falling forward, trying to catch my breath.

His hands continued pushing my bottom into him until he froze in his release, teeth clenched, and fingers dug into my skin. Only a dramatic exhale escaped his lips from the climax. Then he wrapped his arms around my body and buried his head in my chest, panting.

It was amazing. We were amazing together. That was the first team-effort sex I'd ever had, and it was so hot.

With a long exhale, he fell back onto the couch, taking me with him while holding me tight.

"Stay with me tonight," I said, hoping to do it all again and again and find other ways to do it.

I'd discover all his sexual tricks and maybe keep him as my prisoner to serve me whenever I required a fix.

"No," he said.

I yanked his head back by his hair to glare into his eyes for defying my order.

"No?" I barked and got off his lap, his now satisfied cock slipping from inside me. He pulled up his underwear and closed his pants in what seemed like a dismissal.

"You got what you wanted, and now it's time for me to go."

His cold attitude railroaded me.

"You're just going to leave?" I scoffed.

He stood and buttoned his shirt. "Yes, Lisa. I'm leaving. You're going to rest now. Maybe have a good night's sleep. Because a line of clothes is due with samples for a trade show, right? Time's a wasting, and there'll be no more distractions from me."

My mouth opened to protest, but nothing came out. I was flabbergasted, still taken aback by his change in demeanor. He was right. We were missing four more pieces to produce before the show. I missed his body heat already. I craved him, but I didn't at the same time. Was it just his body? Maybe? I liked our conversations too. He was funny, cool, and had great taste in fashion.

He kissed my forehead. "Get some rest, princess."

Then he walked away, leaving me dripping in his juices and half-naked in my freezing living room.

When the front door shut, I couldn't move. Was I mad or relieved?

Leaving my dress on the couch and the dirty dishes in the sink, I locked the front door, climbed the stairs, and entered my slate-tiled bathroom with the large Jacuzzi tub—a luxury that made me buy this house.

I loved the tub at my mother's house, and I concluded that more women should design homes because the Jacuzzi tub should be standard like a garage. My brain deserved a pause. Tomorrow, I'll plan and worry about tomorrow. A bath was the solution for right now.

I watched the water pour from the two faucets and four side tubes starting to steam. I pushed the lever to close the drain, then grabbed two large towels from the back of the door.

Laundry. Got to do laundry. Maybe I'd call Maria to help me out once a week. All right. I cheered myself. That was it, effective planning to make my life better.

Satisfied with my clear thinking and a solution to several problems, I happily stripped off my underwear and sank into the scalding tub.

*Heaven.*

It'd been weeks since I'd indulged in my sanctuary; my beautiful bathroom was open, light, and super modern. I took the lighter from the far side of the tub, lit my lavender candles, and shouted to Alexa in my bedroom to play my spa playlist.

My head was clearing from the putrid smoke of my dumpster-fire life and turning into lavender-scented steam, lifting into the air of my quiet space devoid of my sports watching husband and Mom's cackling coven. This was *my* space. I was ready to get organized for the show now.

Ben had given me so much more than just an orgasm. I had new clarity in my tormented mind to get things done, ready to take matters into my own hands and resolved to the fact I was all alone in doing so. I'd get those samples done and save my company, my name, and my sanity.

# Chapter Six

*Ben*

*Bang, bang, bang, bang.*

"Fuck. Fuck. Fuuuuuck."

My lovely debutante could be heard from outside the warehouse. I smiled. She was angrier than me at that moment.

And I was pretty angry because I'd just met with my parole officer, an ex-marine who didn't believe in rehabilitation for criminals. He was all buzz cut and black-rimmed glasses, ramrod posture, and unforgiving silences. Nick Laudermann was waiting for me to fuck up again because California was a 'three-strikes' state, and with another violation, I'd be sent up for at least twenty years.

"What did you do to make sure you contributed to society in the past month, Ben?" He didn't lay his eyes on me.

Instead, he perused the file on his desk. No computer. Nick didn't believe in technology. He was just a jerk and lived to provoke me every time I'd had to see him for the past six years. Today, I was going to be chill because I'd already put in the paperwork for a personnel transfer. I'd get a new officer appointed in a week. *Hasta la vista, mutherfucker.*

After I was fired by Marisol's father, Hector, Nick went ballistic on me for losing another job. I'd appeased him by using Dad's Camry to drive for a ride-sharing service a few nights a week.

Seeing the meeting on my calendar Sunday night after leaving Lisa's with her taste still on my lips made me decide to change a few things to make my life a little sunnier. Firing Nick Laudermann was the first step.

I hadn't seen her in two days, but I could still feel her pussy clamp down on my dick when she came. I would've stayed with her. I would've kept her in bed for days, tasting her *Sweetart* lips. Just thinking about it made my tongue seep saliva, almost making me drool.

I followed the ruckus to the design room where she was pounding on the long green table with a rubber mallet, head down and teeth clenched into a sneer.

Her other hand was in the air, her thumb bright red and starting to swell.

"Better let her finish," the familiar raspy voice of Dottie came from behind me. "I raised three girls. Believe me, this fit she's having is best left alone."

"What the hell?" Jason appeared, and we all watched Lisa have her way with the table outside the room, giving her some space.

"How long has she been doing that?" he asked Dottie as the banging and profanity continued.

Tearful murmurs came from the crazed woman wielding the deadly weapon.

"About five minutes." Dottie threw her hands up and walked away.

"Well, that should do it." He inched into the room with his hands raised in surrender.

He approached Lisa like she was a scared, caged tiger. Then he slid the mallet from her hand and took her against his chest, letting her sob. My muscles tensed from watching him hold her. My skin burned. It should be me comforting her.

"Hey, sexy," Dottie called to me from a towering machine with stacked rollers and a large arm with a knife that ran the length of it. "Come here. I wanna show you how to use a pattern machine."

"I-I don't think—" I stared at the doorway where my princess was crying.

"I'm not going to be around forever, stud. Lisa won't use it. Hates the thing. So, now you've got to learn," Dottie said.

"What makes you think I'll be any good?" I asked in confusion.

"Anyone is better than her."

With a sigh, I headed over to Dottie, casting a last glance at Jason and Lisa. I guess it was better than just staring at them, imagining grabbing Jason by the neck, and throwing him aside so I could scoop up Lisa myself.

Yeah, better I work with Dottie.

She placed her crooked finger on the keypad and pushed a button with an image of a shirt. The screen showed several images of short and long sleeves, then the body of a solid shirt and a button-down.

"Make your choice." Her boney finger pressed a button-down shirt image, long sleeve, "Then the specs. The codes are here." I squinted my eyes at an old, yellowed piece of paper taped above the screennames like 'Henley,' 'Baggy,' 'slim pant,' 'Slim T,' etc.

"That seems easy and quick." I tried to be polite but felt like she was patronizing me.

I was met with a hard glare. "That's not the hard part, slick," she barked, ending with a wheeze.

I waited to see if she'd have a coughing fit.

When she didn't, she led me into the design room. "It makes the patterns, but you've got to cut them out here."

I followed the woman. Lisa met my gaze, a frown darkening her face, then she peered at the table again.

Was she mad at me for leaving the other night? Did she regret what we'd done? I didn't. But I couldn't stay. Deep down, she would've hated me for it if I had. Getting her head right was essential. I knew that from experience.

The responsibility was on her shoulders to bring the company back from disaster. With her head clear and a good night's sleep, she could make it right.

So much was riding on her mental state to reach her goal and steer the ship that she'd been manning in her father's absence, I didn't want to be in her way. There would be resentment in the long run I couldn't bear. So I left.

Shifting things on the table, she tugged a T-shirt from the bottom of the pile, then handed it to Jason, whose face dropped.

"We can't use this image," he said. "I'd been through this with your mother twenty-five years ago."

"What is it?" I asked, and he tossed me the shirt from the other side of the table. I opened the shirt to see the familiar image of the Grim Reaper riding a wave and the words I hadn't read in a lifetime. "The surf in hell was all right, but the surf in Huntington was better."

"This is the Eaters logo." I shuddered.

The notorious Huntington Cliffs gang that had beaten kids for surfing their territory was staring at me like the many bad decisions I'd made in my youth.

This image reminded me of the one I'd regretted the most. "Jason's right. You can't use this."

"I can do whatever the fuck I want. We own the copyright to that image."

Her words sent a shockwave to my core. Anger burst like

dynamite. "Did you make any money off of it?" I gritted my teeth.

"No, we didn't produce the shirts. Now I know why." Lisa glared at Jason.

"I told your mom any kid wearing that shirt would get their ass kicked. She shouldn't be responsible for it. Besides, none of the shops would buy it for that reason," he said.

I seethed.

A loud snap resounded, like a log breaking in a campfire.

I glanced down. I had gripped the side of the table so hard I'd broken the attached ruler. Jagged and messy, the pieces splintered in my hand.

"What the hell, Ben?" Lisa roared.

"I drew that," I growled; the pain of the splinters was nothing compared to the white-hot rage inside me. "How come nobody asked me if you could use it?"

"I-I just saw the mural when I was a teenager and snapped a photo of it. My mom liked it and got a graphic artist to produce a copy." She gasped. "Shit, you drew this? You were an Eater?"

I exhaled and tried to put the pieces of the ruler back in place.

A flash of memory hit me hard. That horrible incident, the one that sent me to jail for beating a kid for the mere wrong choice of surfing at a public beach in an ocean belonging to no one.

I jerked off my shirt and turned around to show them my most prominent tattoo across my back from shoulder to shoulder; I had the Reaper blacked out to a shadow stick figure. Still, the image was decipherable through the cover-up—just one of many mistakes.

I rubbed the back of my neck, licked my dry lips, and turned around. My heart pounded, but I owed Jason and Lisa an explanation. "I was an Eater, but that was a long time ago. It wasn't… I went to jail for beating up some kid, then my buddy Cullen died, and the group disbanded."

They were staring at me. I smoothed my shirt back down.

"I'm sorry, Ben. I didn't know. I just thought it was a cool image," Lisa choked on her words, her face turning gray like an invisible hand was tightening around her throat.

"Yeah. So did I." I sighed.

A shooting pain hit me in the chest at her heartbroken expression. How could I erase the past five minutes? I'd crushed her dreams. I wouldn't ever want to do that.

She rounded the table and stood close enough to me that she had to cock her head back like she had on the beach, pleading with her big brown eyes.

Her puppy dog look wasn't a ruse. She was desperate. "I'm sorry that happened. I'm truly sorry for all of it. Ben, it's the only image we own outright, and we don't have the time or resources to negotiate another one before the show. Tennent has to have a T-shirt. It's our legacy, and this is amazing." She picked up the T-shirt and shook it. "I'll pay you royalties when we can, but please, please, let us use it."

"Why even ask me? No one asked me back then." I was still upset. I wouldn't have seen a dime if they'd used the image and made millions of dollars.

Her shoulders tensed, and she shook her beautiful head. "We didn't know. I didn't know, but now we can draw up a formal agreement."

She was pleading with my soul, which was already so close to being hers. This woman could do or ask anything from me. I exhaled and took a step back before I ran my fingers through her hair.

"Please, Ben. I need you to say yes. Please."

In that Princess Leia moment, my mouth watered. I better not drool thinking of her Sweetart lips. My muscles were constricting, stopping me from taking her in my arms. This would be another path to becoming her hero if I said yes.

"Would you see the guys and find out if they're cool about it? I don't want any scuffles because of this image on a T-shirt," Jason added, snapping me out of my staring contest with Lisa.

"No, it was all me." I glanced at him, then at Lisa. "Fine, we'll give it a shot and see if the stores buy it. There are probably just a few old guys who remember anyway."

She put her swollen thumb to her lip and turned away from me.

"If we could go to each shop and make the wording for each town, like custom. 'The surf at Trestles' 'The surf in Hermosa' 'The surf in Malibu'" She waved a hand. "You know what I mean? Those towns probably don't know or care about the reputation of the Eaters, and it's a great image, Ben."

It was an inspiring idea. She'd done it again with her vision—such a hottie.

"I love it." Brad entered the room. "Finally, something to sell. Oh, and I could do a road trip up and down the coast and see the stores."

"You're trying to escape from Kelly and the baby for a while. Admit it," she quipped at her brother. "And surf," she added as she flung a hat at him.

He made a face so woe-is-me, I nearly laughed aloud. He answered with a man-baby whine, "If I get thrown up on one more time, I'm going to lose it. Kelly's post-partum is off the charts. How'd you deal with it, man?" He held his hand out to Jason, our elder.

"None of it bothered me with Jasmine. She was cute even when she was yacking on me. Gabby didn't have any post-partum. She just went on like it was nothing. So, sorry, I can't help you there."

Brad leaned on the table next to me. "You ever been married, Ben?"

All gazes shot to me.

I squirmed a bit but tried not to let it show.

"Engaged for a while. We've got a kid too, but Marisol and I never pulled the trigger. Nope," I answered.

I'd just met all these people. Why did I have to be so honest with them, telling them my fucking life story? Not that it wasn't printed on my body. My tats were like hieroglyphics at this point. All anyone had to do was piece it together. Easier said than done because some days, even I had trouble piecing my life together.

Brad sighed and pushed himself from the table. I hadn't noticed he was holding a rolled-up poster in his hand until he threw it on the table and began to unroll it. Lisa joined him on the other side, taking her electricity with her, leaving me dizzy and sad.

"Jason," he said, "Will you approve this?"

Jason ran his hands over the large image, flattening it out so she could place giant metal scissors on one side and a tape measure on the other. We all took it in.

The image was stunning. A photo of a dark silhouette standing on the shore, the water reflecting an orange and pink sunset with "Jason Mattis for Tennent Surf Co." printed across it. There was something so mystical about it, like witnessing a legendary warrior returning to save the universe, but with a surfboard.

"It's awesome. Really. Gus would love it," Jason said.

Maybe it was because I was paying so much attention to Lisa, but at the name, she stiffened—a small thing. I'm surprised I noticed it. Then again, ever since I set eyes on that woman, I seem to be attentive to every damn thing about her. She *had* reacted when Jason said her father's name.

I was about to tell Jason to take it back, apologize, and switch places so I could be next to her.

I didn't do any of that. He kept staring at the poster; he loved being the focus of the new and resurrected company, excited to be the superstar again. His hand covered his mouth in a moment of humility. A small chuckle and plastered smile showed pure elation.

"How many posters?" she asked her brother.

"Two thousand. We'll bring a few hundred to the show for Jason to sign. Oh, and Jason, they also asked for you to sit on the press panel with other surf champions. They haven't said who's confirmed yet. Things are a bit different now," he added with a roll of his eyes. "They all have Hollywood-type agents and managers these days."

"Shoot me if I ever get an agent," Jason quipped. "Those guys are sleazier than lawyers. Don't tell my wife that."

Lisa was grinning, and she almost seemed light. The electric glow crackled in her eyes, but it was yellow and bright as sunshine this time. If I made her cheeks blush with lust, she could be a rainbow again—a new goal.

As if she could hear my thoughts, her gaze flicked to me. A lightning bolt damn near hit me.

She studied the poster again. "This is it. Just a few little things like order sheets, although I don't expect to get any at the show, and a few more pieces for the line, We are going to have the biggest buzz." She held her hand out to our hero. "And the triumphant return of Jason 'The Zen Shredder' Mattis."

Brad and Dottie clapped, and Jason bowed like he accepted the honor with grace.

"Oh, I should make social media posts and call the magazines." Lisa trotted past me and squeezed my hand. That little gesture made me itch to follow her to the office and give her a little afternoon lick under her desk.

"Okay, let's go, Ben." Jason interrupted my boss-woman fantasy. "We've got to grab some stuff from my dad's house and the storage unit for my old boards."

I hoped I had a bit to do with Lisa's better mood. My new mission in life was to make her life sunshine and rainbows again.

~ * ~

Peach-flavored Arizona iced tea gurgled up my throat as Jason turned off PCH into the former dirt parking lot, now paved with parking payment machines. The sign read "Huntington Cliffs Dog Beach,' not the 'scene of my demise."

The Cliffs was the location of my humiliating arrest after we'd jumped a kook surfer we deemed didn't belong. I found out later that he lived right off 17th Street, blocks away. We didn't care. The cliffside adorned my notorious mural with 'Kirk,' the surfing Reaper from hell. The Eaters owned this beach a long time ago.

Jason grinned at me.

I glared at him. "Why here?"

"Karma," he answered with a sardonic smile before hopping from the car. He threw my wetsuit through my window, hitting me square in the face, then went to the back of the truck. "Come on, kook."

I growled. Jason was enjoying this way too much.

Being there again was jarring. So much shame came with this place. I sat for another minute, mustering my strength to face it. I was sulking in the cab of Jason's truck staring at the rustic wood railing of the boardwalk. People walked their dogs and rode bikes on the path that stretched south to the Huntington Pier, having no idea about the emotional crisis I was dealing with.

I finally got out and met him at the tailgate to put on our wetsuits. I left mine hanging around my waist and took off my shirt.

More silence as we hooked our boards under our arms and headed to the opening in the railing at the lifeguard stand. Jason stopped at the pay kiosk, and I mused about how twenty-five years ago we would've beaten that thing with lead pipes before we'd pay to park at our beach.

"Shit. Is that Jason Mattis?" an old guy sitting at a small table under an umbrella shouted.

He had a silver beard, razor sunglasses, and one of those big woven surf hats. A crude posterboard sign read: "Say no to immigrants." In several colors, it went on in the sloppy handwritten text: "Stop illegals from taking our jobs."

There had been protesters here since the 1960s calling for the dismantling of monstrously huge offshore oil rigs visible from the Cliffs and the north side of Huntington Pier. People hated them. Every few years, a spill would get into the surf, making surfers and sea life ill and eroding the reef. I'd never witnessed this type of protest—the angry hate of actual people.

Jason sauntered to the old dude and shook his hand. I didn't join him, trying to avoid an altercation with an obvious bigot. Instead, I headed for the broken cement block hill down to the sand.

"Holy shit. Is that Big Ben?" the man shouted at my back, maybe recognizing my tattoo.

I stopped as the air left my lungs. Only one person called me that. The one who let me take the fall for our gang jumping an innocent and sending me to jail at eighteen—Pete 'Morbius' Mulholland. He'd given himself the name. What an asshole.

I turned with a scowl. If Jason wasn't giving me a pleading look, I would've tackled the fucker and beat the ever-loving shit out of him. Instead, I counted to ten in my head as my teeth ground, but my lips curled up in a fake smile.

"Pete. Long time." I sounded pissed, and I wasn't upset about it.

He should know what I thought about him and his fucking sign.

I imagined beating him over the head with it. Instead, I stayed where I was, counting, so I wouldn't let violence take over.

He grinned and said, "Hey, wait up a minute. I'll hit the swell with you."

Fuck. That was the last thing I wanted. Sure, he was no longer a punk, but he remained a treasonous backstabber and an immigrant hater. I counted to twenty.

He picked up an old shredder board leaning on the railing behind him. When he took the hat and sunglasses off, I saw the twenty-year-old face I used to call my friend. He was golden-tanned but had gray eyebrows and hair in place of the Irish orange locks he and his brother Cullen had shared.

I was closer to Cullen, who'd passed away in 1997 from an anaphylactic allergy to shellfish during a surf trip to Baja. I, of course, heard about it second-hand. I stayed far away from the other gang members after my parole and Cliffs, until now.

Pete huffed as he caught up to us. I gingerly went down the rocks to the sand as he and Jason engaged in small talk. Trying not to show any friendliness to Pete, I waited for them, and we all attached our leashes around our ankles, silently wading into the waves.

My head echoed visual memories of the oil rigs in the distance and the chatter among the gang as we bobbed on our boards, waiting for a wave. I only wanted to hang out with Jason. Like Pete always had a knack for, he ruined everything, just like he's ruining the moment and my mood.

Two young men sat on their boards nearby, and Jason, being Jason, started a conversation. They spoke Spanish, and Jason easily switched to their language. As if being a surf god wasn't enough, the man could speak five languages.

I shook my head in amazement.

Pete leaned over to me and spoke in a hushed tone. "Those boys should know better than to surf here."

Could he be that daft? Hadn't the years and my prison time taught him a lesson? This beach didn't belong to anyone.

"They'd best be moving down to the Southside of the Pier or something," Pete grumbled. "You know, with the other illegals."

I rolled my eyes, about to say something, when a swell came toward us. He and one of the boys went after it.

Pete popped up like the old expert he was and sliced right across the younger man's board, knocking him off.

Jason tsked his tongue and shook his head.

"Same ol,' same ol'," he lamented, then paddled to catch the next wave.

Pete returned to my side and let out a breath. His smile was nauseating and ugly. "Next time, I'm going to be more convincing."

"Just surf, man," I said. "Check your vibes, and let it go."

He glared at me. "Oh, yeah, Big Ben? That's what they teach you in jail? Vibes and shit?"

Jason joined us and glanced at me, then at Pete.

The air thickened between him and me. Overcast skies started to break into sunshine streams, and the fins of a school of dolphins passed in front of us. The younger men gushed and pointed.

We sat like statues. The glorious sight before us was overshadowed by too much tension.

I finally chased a wave, getting a reprieve from Pete and his lousy karma, realizing how toxic that vibe was.

This was the classic Huntington Cliffs slow roll I loved—long, steady, and soothing. An old guy on a longboard hung ten a few feet away in his big straw hat, his face a picture of calm and Zen. I saw my future in that guy.

Then dropping down, I turned back to see Pete with his hands flailing as he spoke to Jason. I approached them just in time to catch Pete's words.

"Those fuckers are gonna ruin this country—" he grumbled. "That's why I won't buy a goddamn computer from them. Then the piece of shit that owns the store asked me to leave. Fucking Jew."

Jason glanced at me, and we shared an exasperated smirk.

Pete took the next wave.

"Asshole," I said.

"He is." Jason shot me a knowing look. "He's an angry, bigoted old man."

"It makes me sick how I used to hang out with him and looked up to him."

"Well, you used to be just as angry."

My eyes widened. "I wasn't some raging racist piece of shit."

"No, I'm sure you weren't. Your anger was directed at yourself. That kind of shit is easier to fix because you've already taken responsibility. You're not blaming everybody and anybody for how your life turned out. Pete… That's all he can do. He's full of that hate." Jason gave me a soft smile. "You're not. You never were."

That made me grin. I'm owning up to my issues. It can be fixed. Now I can help Lisa with hers if she'd let me.

"I'm lucky you came into my life, man. I—"

I didn't finish my heartfelt speech to my brother when Pete

returned.

We didn't talk much after that because the swell got three-tiered, and everyone was catching some epic waves—one after the other.

After a few hours, my arms were sore, and I needed a nap. Jason, being fifty-four, should have been dead. He wasn't. He was a fucking livewire, and I swear he could've gone for another three hours. We all knew it was time to go and paddled toward the shore. Even the two younger men came in with us.

Jason hung back with them, laughing, and joking in Spanish when four tatted and jacked men approached.

"Get them Beaners off the beach." A shaved head with a swastika tattoo on his clavicle barked, pointing at the men.

*Huntington Nazis.* Unfortunately, not a new thing. Dread filled my stomach with fluttering contractions, just like I felt when I was about to fight.

Pete approached the punks. "Come on, Riley. This is Jason Mattis. The fucking legend. Don't start shit with him."

Swastika boy growled. His anger was a lit fuse about to ignite, and a chill raced up my spine.

"I told you to call me Rage, Uncle Pete," he said.

"Fine, *Rage*." Pete dragged out the nickname sarcastically. "Show some respect for Jason, and my old friend Ben, here. They both got out and did something with themselves."

His characterization of me was unfounded. The only time I'd left Huntington was when I went to Santa Ana Central Men's Jail.

"Fuck you, old man." Another punk spat at Pete. "You sticking up for these wetbacks?" He pointed to the young men now behind me. I was a bigger wall of protection than Jason.

But then one of the young guys piped up in perfect English and loud enough for the Nazis to hear. He shouted, "Who are you calling names, *Riley*?"

Shit.

Before I knew it, the Nazi charged me—a big mistake. I'd learned mixed martial arts in prison. I'd always thought it wasn't such a good idea to teach violent criminals fighting techniques, but I enjoyed it. The way he advanced was all wrong, and I had the advantage.

When he reached me, I threw my shoulder into his belly and flipped him behind me with an 'oof' escaping his mouth as his back hit the hard wet sand. He had the wind knocked out of him. I recognized the expulsion of air. Then he doubled over and lay on his side.

I turned to the others.

"Anyone else want to come at me?" I squatted into a wrestling pose with my arms stretched out and waved my fingers in a taunt.

We were in the clear when they walked past us with sneers and grumbles.

"That's your nephew, huh?" Jason asked Pete.

"Yeah, my sister's kid. He's kind of an asshole."

I snorted—the pot calling the kettle black.

We picked up our boards and climbed the rocks to the lifeguard stand.

The lifeguard, a young woman with a big smile, said, "That was epic, Zen Shredder. Come back any time with your friend."

We laughed and started toward Jason's truck. We bid the youngsters goodbye, and Pete wandered back to his umbrella.

"That was epic, Zen Shredder," I teased in a high-pitched voice.

Jason laughed. "Not my fault. I still got it."

"Jay, I didn't finish telling you—"

He stopped me with a hand up. "You'll figure out your way, Ben. Just know you're on the right path. You're my brother, for real." With that, he nodded, and I didn't have to say another word. My brother had my back.

We wrapped towels around our waists and pulled the wetsuits down underneath. It's more complicated than it looks. Cullen and I'd practiced in my driveway for weeks when I was thirteen to ensure we didn't seem like kooks when we got to the beach.

Jason leaned on his tailgate while he did it, teaching me a new trick.

I slipped my dry shorts under the towel, and when the towel dropped, there was applause and whoops from a group of bikini-clad girls behind us. My shorts had barely made it over my ass, and I had an audience.

The girls kept their distance but muttered, "Oh, daddy" and "Silver fox."

Jason must be used to it. He closed the tailgate and went to the truck's cab while I fumbled with my drawstrings and strained to hear more of what the girls were saying.

"Come on, Daddy Ben," he shouted as the truck roared to life.

My cheeks burned when I joined him.

"You still got it, old man," he teased.

I smiled and chuckled too.

# Chapter Seven

*The Triple S Show*
*San Diego Convention Center, San Diego, CA*
*Lisa*

Standing in front of our meager twenty-foot booth, we frowned. "It's so fucking small," Brad complained.

I wasn't going to acknowledge his bitching, but a slight growl came from somewhere inside me.

Tennent had put the Triple S Trade Show on the map back in the day, and the organizers offered Dad carte blanche to have him be a part of it in the 1990s. Huge corner spots with free designers and builders to make the space a destination for all of the buyers from big and small stores carrying surf, skate, and snow clothing. One year, we had bikini-clad models handing out stickers. Mom put a stop to that.

Another year, we'd had a local band play on a makeshift stage then a fashion show. In other years, we'd sponsored not only Jason but two or more champion surfers as our team. Poster signing had fans and buyers lining up to give us orders.

No models now. No local band. No two or more champion surfers. Just a tiny booth in the back, hidden and unremarkable.

Jason was there, thank God, which was a big ace up our sleeve. *But still.*

"It has potential," his wife, Shelly, said, placing a consoling hand on my shoulder.

"Potential? My fucking ass." My fists clenched, and the skin on the back of my neck started to burn up to my ears. I shouted, "This isn't twenty by forty."

She winced. Maybe I would've done the same at my outburst, too, but I was too damn upset. I opened my bag and fished for the order sheets. I had too much shit in there, and I couldn't find the sheets, so I just flipped the purse upside down and poured everything out.

Brad, Shelly, and Kelly stood around me like street cones so I wouldn't get run over by the carts, people carrying bins, and rolling racks with extensive summer lines of at least twenty clothing pieces.

I finally found what I was searching for and stood to see two adorable young girls pushing racks full of samples. In contrast, Brad had six pieces on our broken, duck-tapped, ancient rack, and my breakfast of avocado toast and fruit almost came up my throat. I felt so outclassed when this place should feel like home.

The overhead sound system blared "Let's Dance," shouted by Kevin Bacon in the movie *Footloose* followed by the theme song echoing in the ample space of the convention center floor—we looked up as if we could see Kevin Bacon himself. The DJ must have spotted Jason. "Let's Dance" was his catchphrase back in his competition days.

My head pounded from the hammering and noise as the larger companies erected their impressive booths, and I stood glaring at our tiny space.

A bare, six-foot folding table was on its side, and two metal chairs were inside.

Brad took the rack into the claustrophobic booth, and Shelly helped me turn the table upright.

Kelly produced a printed tablecloth out of a bin and handed it to me. It was the same image as the poster with Jason's name and would sit at the mouth of the booth for him to sign posters. The two chairs were for the buyers, and the rest of us would have to linger outside in the aisle because it would be too tight of a squeeze.

"Footloose" ended and "Let's Dance" by David Bowie started. A crowd marched down the aisle toward us, led by The Zen Shredder himself. It was amazing to hear the show celebrate Jason's return but even more amazing to see how the crowd responded. They understood what that song meant and who it was meant for.

Shelly's hands flew to her cheeks, and her eyes welled up. The emotion at the memory of her husband's superstar status and the collective respect he garnered even though he'd been away for twenty years was overwhelming me too. I had another layer, vindication. Tennent Surf was going to rule this trade show from our tiny booth buried in the back of the San Diego Convention Center.

Echoes of multiple people laughing came toward us. I peered to the end of the aisle to where Jason stood surrounded by people with phones snapping his picture and others holding them up to catch his words. He was talking and smiling.

Shelly crossed her arms. "Well, he's going to be impossible after all this attention."

I would have laughed if I wasn't so stressed.

The entourage approached.

"There she is." Jason pointed, and I thought he was motioning to Shelly, his new wife, and the famous romance writer, M.R. Taylor.

But he took my hand and drew me in front of the group whose cameras turned to me.

I caught Ben's eye, towering over the reporters, standing out of place with all his tattoos and imposing presence with no phone camera up to my face like the others.

"Lisa, how did you get Jason to come back?" a petite blond guy asked me.

I scoffed. "That's a weird question."

All stared at me, waiting for an answer, and I realized I had to make nice. I conjured my cotillion days and mustered up my debutante smile. Then put my hand on Jason's shoulder.

"Well, it was all his idea. He was back from Brazil and gave us a call. Of course, we wanted him back. Are you kidding?" I giggled, but on the inside, I was gagging.

I wasn't comfortable with public speaking. I'd gotten that from Dad. That was why he'd loved Jason so much.

Someone else spoke up. "Jason, I hear you're designing a clothing line for older, more sophisticated surfers?"

He chuckled, then asked the tall, gray-haired man, "Who you calling old, Darren? If I remember your twenty-first birthday in Miami…"

The group laughed.

Brad jumped in, thank goodness. The last thing I needed was any more questions directed at me.

"It's like a quality line of men's fashion but with a surfer's appeal. We're going to keep the prices moderate for everyone. Ben, come show them." He waved Ben from the crowd.

I wasn't sure that was a good idea with him wearing the flannel jacket over the Eater's shirt and looked so delicious, I almost wrapped my arms around him and bit his neck.

Ben took the jacket off, showed the reporters the grommeted air holes, and gave me credit for the idea, turning to me with a wink. I visualized tearing his clothes off. Then he showed off his design on the back of the T-shirt. The pictures snapped. He also didn't take credit for the image of the Reaper surfer. Well, there was modesty, then there was entirely not taking any credit. Time to interject. I pushed forward and pointed to the image.

"This is Ben Stringer, and he designed this logo from an old surf gang. Isn't it sick?"

He first glanced at me over his shoulder in terror, then his expression changed into something I couldn't place.

"Ben, do you have other designs?" one woman asked, a bit too flirty for my taste, and I may have scowled at her.

"Uh, y-yeah, tons, but you'll have to wait for them." He nodded to me. "This is all about Jason's summer line at the show."

"That's right," Brad chimed in again. "The Eaters shirts will be exclusive to the local surf shops with the option to put their surf spot on the graphic."

*Oohs* and *ahhs* followed Brad's statement. He glowed like it was his idea and his alone. That didn't matter. We were a team, and every little piece of the press would serve our greater goal.

We had taken up the entire aisle, and a backup of rolling racks was stretched to the end, unable to get through because of our impromptu press conference.

Two large security officers shouted to clear the space, and the crowd thinned, having gotten their story.

A stocky man about Dad's age strolled like a king down the aisle, and the sea parted. Andrew Portocolis, the owner of the company that put the show on, held a young woman's hand. She was dressed a bit too Beverly Hills for our laid-back little convention, wearing sky-high Louboutins that she'd regret after a few hours of walking the cement floor.

"What is this?" Ben leaned over to my ear, and the heat of his breath did things to my panty area.

"Andy the Greek," I said softly.

"Jason Mattis." Andy shook hands with the legend. "It's awesome to have you here, man."

As Andy and Jason talked, Ben led me over to the far side of our booth and stared at me. His eyes were getting darker.

"That was kind of a rush," he whispered in my ear, giving me chills.

He stepped away, and the look returned. The one I couldn't read. Was it lust, admiration, or frustration? Did he want to throw me off a cliff or kiss me? I didn't have time to figure it out because Jason called me over to him.

Andy's lady friend was now gushing all over Shelly, and Jason motioned with his hand out to draw me closer.

"Andy has a suggestion." Jason smiled at me with a bit of smugness.

I was already 0-for-1 on reading men's expressions and was worried about losing control of this situation. It seemed the men were in charge, and I needed to wrangle back my authority. Since he asked, I listened to Andy.

"Your location is proving to be a logistical nightmare if this continues, so I'm moving your booth."

I peered up at Jason, who nodded.

"Awesome," Brad sang.

"Uh, where? I mean, you're not going to kick someone else out of their space, are you?" I eyed the corner spot like we used to have.

"We were going to make a lounge in the front along the south wall, but that space would be better used to keep traffic flow to the perimeters." He tapped on his phone.

I peered at my grinning men, and a rush of love warmed my insides for the three of them, which was weird because I hated men. They were useless. Weren't they?

We brought our supplies to the front doors of the show floor, and in the left corner was a cozy little area with tan suede couches facing each other surrounding two rustic, polished teak coffee tables. The space was cool and Zen, and my heart leaped once, then beat so fast I had to take a few deep breaths.

"It's fantastic. We can put our banners on the wall and have a table for Jason," Brad gushed.

My team started unpacking. Panic hit me. How much was this going to cost? We'd practically blown through Jason's cash infusion with nothing to show for it yet.

I leaned closer to Andy. "Uh, how much more are you going to charge us?"

Andy stepped away from me and started laughing with his whole body, then walked away with his girl toy wrapped around his arm.

Well, that was that. He wasn't going to tell me, and I wouldn't stress about it.

I faced the cozy, beautifully appointed space, and excitement enraptured me. Ben and Brad were chatting as they leaned old surfboards against the wall, and I was happy for the first time in recent memory. This was going to work and put us back on the map. Dad would be thrilled.

At the thought of him, my happiness dimmed. Not gone completely, but my full-wattage joy dipped. His absence was a void and one that was able to drain all good feelings down into it. He better have a damn good reason for leaving us.

But I couldn't think about that now. We had the welcome party that night, and tomorrow was the triumphant return of Tennent Surf and our Jason Mattis, The Zen Shredder.

~ * ~

"Mick Jagger said, 'you can't dress like a hobo until you spend a lot of cash,'" Kelly announced and sipped her frothy pink drink from a martini glass like she'd made the statement of the century.

I figured she'd be a lightweight after two drinks since my baby nephew was only ten months old, and they didn't get out much. *She was.*

Shelly and Jason fell back, groaning.

"Ugh, millennials," Shelly lamented.

"Not the right words," Jason added. "But Billy Joel said that."

"No way. Not the 'Uptown Girl' guy." Kelly scanned each of our faces. "He didn't sing that. He's too sweet. It had to be Mick Jagger or someone like that."

"Like what?" Jason interjected.

"You know, more badass," Brad chimed in.

We were in a corner at a club in the Gaslamp district for the welcome party of the show. The Greek had come by to make sure we approved of our new space, and I still didn't trust that I'd get a bill for ten grand next week.

"Listen, kids." Jason put his elbows on his knees. "Billy Joel was a motorcycle-riding, chain-smoking, swearing, drunk when he first started. He was the epitome of a badass. 'Still Rock and Roll to Me' was a great song from a great album. 'Uptown Girl' was an unfortunate product of him trying to fit in with a *tonier* society."

"Great word, babe." Shelly squeezed Jason's knee.

That made me sit forward and glance at Ben next to me. I craved his hand on my knee, leg, stomach, breasts, ass, and everywhere else. He winked when I caught his eye.

"What does 'tonier' mean?" he asked.

He was sitting back with his arms stretched out over the back of the couch like the night at my house when he'd given me a wonderful gift, then left. His one arm behind me made me want to snuggle into his warm body, but I'd made sure not to lean into him.

Even though the more I drank my strong margarita and inhaled his distinct scent of leather and citrus, the thoughts of us groping each other in full view got more vivid.

Jason had his hand on Shelly's knee, and Brad sat like Ben but with one arm around his wife's back. He petted her hair and intermittently stroked her back.

Would Ben ever do that with me? We had sex once with no indication we ever would again. He dashed out the door before we'd discussed what we'd done or what it had meant. That same feeling of confusion and relief consumed me. I was curious, but at the same time, I wasn't.

We were becoming friends, and he seemed determined to see me truly happy. He'd even recognized how stressed out I was about the last piece for the line. When I'd come into the design room last Friday, a pattern and unique sketch for a pair of plaid pants with hidden zipper cargo pockets was waiting for me. It was his style and similar to a pair he'd worn a few times, maybe another of his designer resale purchases.

There was no denying it. The sexual spark was there between us, for sure. My itch had been scratched, and he'd selflessly seen to that without expecting or asking for more. Somehow, he knew my need to focus on the show trumped any sexual desire. It was building though, having him so close.

"Tonier means upper class, high society," Shelly explained.

A collective 'oh,' rang from us.

We talked more about musicians and rock bands for a while longer before Jason stood.

"Okay," he announced, tugging Shelly from the low couch, "time to go. Big day tomorrow." He raised his glass with barely a swallow in it. "To resurrections!"

We cheered to that and drank.

"Night all," he said, wrapping his wife in his arms as they crossed the dance floor, disappearing into the crowd.

Kelly sighed and smiled. "He's amazing, and Shelly too. I had no idea she was M.R. Taylor, *and* she's your sister, Ben? That's so exciting."

All I could think was, 'make her stop talking.' She was a beautiful blonde with a cherub face and a lean body. She was the kind of pretty that wouldn't have to work a day in her life, and I wasn't surprised that she was the kind of girl my brother married.

Society probably saw me as just like her once upon a time, raised for polite conversation and planning dinner parties. Some charity work and shopping. That was my life for eleven years. I glared at her. No. I was always darker and more intelligent than that. I just forgot my worth for a while.

Ben's voice sounded in my ear. It made my toes curl, my heart flutter, and chills break out all over.

"Wanna dance?" he asked.

He stood and held his hand out.

I froze. This gesture was in the open for my brother and Kelly to see, clear as day.

To dance and do more with Ben? Yes, I did. He was engaging and thoughtful. Still, he'd gone to jail and had a daughter he hardly saw, as long as I'd known him anyway. Mom would freak out. Dad wouldn't like it at all. What about my Tennent team? Jason? Tina?

Even though I barely knew Shelly, I still valued her opinion. Would she be okay with me for her brother? Was it like Ben was saying, "Are you ready to tell them all to go to hell and take a chance?"

He leaned down, taking my hand. "It's just dancing, Lisa. Chill out and stop thinking so much."

Was that a challenge?

"Let's dance," Brad shouted and broke the tension.

He jumped up, taking Kelly with him, and we all hit the dance floor. Ben moved toward me, backing me up until the crowd swallowed Brad and Kelly.

Ben kept moving closer with that same expression on his face. The one that was making my brain swim and my pussy clench. It was too dark to see his eyes because they were almost black. I kept backing up as he pushed forward until I hit the wall. He pressed against me.

My breath increased at the tension he'd put on my chest. He nudged my legs apart with his knee. Then he put one arm on the wall over my head, and his other hand slowly lifted until his fingertips grazed the underside of my breast. Brushing back and forth, then up to where he assumed my nipple was under my top and circled his feather-light fingers, sending sparks down to my sex.

"Are you drunk?" I asked, trying to lower the temperature between us.

It didn't work. He tipped my chin up with one hand and rubbed harder on my nipple with the other. Then leaned in and shadowed my lips with his. Just as light and slow as his fingers on my fully erect nipple.

"Yes," he hissed. "And I want you."

I tried to gasp, but his lips were already on mine. Damn. He tasted like whiskey and proclivities. He'd let me take control last time, but I wasn't in control this time.

Too many things were happening at once. He'd moved from my lips to my neck while grinding his knee to my aching crotch. Thoughts of his past kept intruding. Yet his kiss, sex, and passion made my brain tread water in the middle of a whirlpool, trying to keep my head from submerging.

We were making out. His touch was absolutely electric. I was about as close to coming as I could be in public during a work party.

Shit.

No, I can't. I can't do this.

I broke the kiss and pushed him away.

~ * ~

*Ben*

Lisa looked lustful, terrified, and angry all at once, my favorite combination on her. It wouldn't last long. Sure as fuck, she dropped her head and started laughing.

Her hands flew up to her face, and she held them there for a few long seconds. I realized then that she wasn't laughing.

"Come on." I took her arm and led her over to the table, grabbed her purse, then dragged her out of the club into the chilly January air. It was past midnight, and groups of loud, drunk people huddled under heat lamps. The laughter and singing faded as we descended the steps to the street. Damn, I could practically hear her heart beating. I turned her toward me, my hand gripping her arm.

Her face was red and tired.

"What's wrong, Lisa?"

"Let go of me," she seethed through clenched teeth and yanked her arm away.

She stared at me in infuriated silence as her chest rose and fell. God, it was frustrating. I was frustrated. All I desired was her, but she wouldn't let me in.

Taking two steps back, I tried to count to ten before shouting at her. She sent me such mixed signals, and my cock was painfully hard.

"You're fighting inside your head right now, and you're taking it out on me." I said.

She sighed. "I'm not taking anything out on you, Ben. I'm leaving you alone. I don't need this right now. Don't you get it?"

"No, I don't get it at all. You want me. Say it." I closed the space between us. "Say it."

She shook her head. "I wanted to fuck you once and get it out of my system. That's it."

"That's not it."

She raised her palms in the air. "That's all I can give you. I'm not in my right mind. Can't you see that? I'm broken. I can't give anymore. Not to you, not to anyone."

Her words hit me like a sledgehammer. Now I knew what was going on. I'd been there my whole life. I had no desire to drag anyone into my hell or let them care about me because I'd fuck it up somehow. How could I make her see that her hell was temporary? She could ascend from it. She was ascending from it already. I recognized it as someone who was so firmly in his own hell.

"Oh, princess." I had to touch her. I had to make her know that I understood so I stroked her cheek. "You're not broken. You're just bent. That's fixable."

She closed her eyes, and hope swelled inside me.

But then she backed away and took a deep breath. "I'm going to take a bath and get a good night's sleep. Alone."

I shoved my hands into my pockets and nodded.

"Okay." I exhaled, and the misty air mixed with my breath. It dissipated on the breeze, and I couldn't help but wonder if our chance to be together was gone, too.

But I couldn't push her. If I did, she'd never let me in, not in her bedroom, arms, or life, and I couldn't bear the thought of that—patience, for the first time in my life. *Count to ten.*

We crossed the street to the W Hotel and went inside. I glanced at her in silence in the elevator. Sadness and disappointment lay between us.

I got off on the fifth floor, and she stayed.

"I'm on the twelfth floor." Her voice shook, and I had no idea whether it was from the chill outside or her decision to let me go alone tonight.

"Good night, then," I said as I started out the doors.

"You're a good person, Ben. Even though we haven't known each other for long, I'm glad to have you on my team."

The words were nice. They should've made me feel good, but she said them like a boss.

My heart sunk. I was part of Team Tennent, for the resurrection. Just like Jason and Brad.

# Chapter Eight



"I forgot what a rush it is to be up there." The Zen Shredder beamed.

Jason was glowing after his Q&A session on the 'Legends' press junket. I was happy for him. He deserved to be recognized for the superstar he was, both as a human and an athlete. We'd all missed his energy. I'd needed his vibes more than I realized.

We meandered to the booth after stopping several times for people to shake his hand or take a picture with him. He was elated, and I basked in the residual glow.

"Lisa." Brad came at me. He was jumping out of his skin. "Betty was just here."

*Oh my god.* My heart thudded against my chest. Betty Morales, the matriarch of Betty's Stores, had been around since the '80s. She'd managed to grow with the change in retail to online shopping and maintain her brand with sixty stores and a multi-million-dollar website commerce business.

And my company got her attention.

Brad and Kelly bounced like kids at Chuck E Cheese. Brad said, "She wants the jacket in all her stores and online. Twelve-hundred pieces. Can you fucking believe it?"

No, I couldn't believe it. As we bounced around and celebrated, realization dawned.

"Wait," I said. "We have a big problem. We can't afford to produce twelve-hundred pieces. We still owe the manufacturer in China, Brad. What the fuck? We'd have to make them here, which will double the price. What were you thinking?"

Shock covered his pretty face.

"So, just do it here," Kelly chimed in.

I couldn't speak. I pictured steam coming from my ears like a cartoon character. As it was, my face was burning, and my blood pressure was escalating through the roof. The twit had no idea what it took to produce that many garments domestically.

"Okay," Brad said, "before you freak out. I have an appointment with Kohl's at three o'clock."

I almost projectile vomited on him. Was he trying to make me combust in the middle of a public place?

"Whaaaaat?" My shout was like an explosion.

Brad and Kelly ducked to avoid any metal debris that might fly at their heads because I went off like a bomb.

I stormed off. *Breathe, breathe, breathe*, my head was saying, but my lungs had seized, and I couldn't outrun the suffocation.

"Lisa," Jason called, but I kept walking.

I doubled my speed past the front doors of the show floor. I still hadn't inhaled. Everything was starting to get hazy. The glass doors to the outside opened, and I stopped under the empty portico.

A tropical depression from Mexico pounded fat raindrops a few feet away, louder than the static in my head.

I ran the numbers in my head for producing the pieces for Betty in L.A. The cost was astronomical. While a Kohl's deal could pay off the Chinese manufacturer if we got an advance from them, we'd just gotten out of the big box shackles, and now we'd have to put them back on.

I took a cigarette from my purse and stuck it between my lips, staring at the rain. The water hitting the asphalt was getting louder in my brain. Before I lit the cancer stick, I stepped out from under the overhang and into the downpour.

This kind of rain wasn't common in Southern California. I was compelled to embrace it every time it poured like this. I didn't give a shit that my hair, makeup, and $700 Gucci sneakers would be ruined.

Fat water drops hit the cigarette I had between my lips, reminding me it was there, and I lifted my hand with the lighter.

"Good luck getting that lit," I heard from behind me and spun to see Ben standing with his hands in the pockets of his baggy shorts—his chain wallet swinging, and his arm tattoos on full display.

I wasn't sure how long I stood there staring at him.

In an act of defiance for him and mother nature, I flicked the metal of the lighter several times. Then threw the damn thing, followed by the cigarette.

"Let me ask you something." He had to shout over the rain, but his tone was calm.

That pissed me off. I was standing in a rainstorm. Soaked from head to toe, I tried to light a cigarette. How in the fucking hell was I qualified to answer any question right now? I hadn't even taken a breath yet.

"Is it about the money? Or is it a fuck you to your old man to prove him wrong about you? Or to fix something that you think is broken?" he asked.

I had to blink to keep the water from getting in my eyes that was now dripping from my forehead.

"That's three questions." I shook my head. "Why are you even out here? What do you care about any of this? Who the fuck are you, Ben?"

He stepped closer. "Now you asked me three questions."

God, he was impossible. What did he think would happen, some romance movie moment in the rain where I jumped into his arms, and we lived happily ever after getting matching tattoos and motorcycles?

In my silence, he answered one of my questions: "I'm Billy-fucking-Joel."

My heart clenched then fell into my stomach. *He knew.*

Of course, he knew what I'd thought last night when Jason described "Uptown Girl" as a man falling in love with a woman out of his world and how it had changed him. Was Ben in love with me? I didn't expect him to change for me. He shouldn't even like me or, God forbid, love me. I wasn't worthy.

"I don't need this shit right now," I shouted at him.

"Answer my question, Lisa."

I wiped the rain from my eyes. "Which one?"

"Is it about the money?"

"Yes, damnit, and my father and fixing broken things. It's all of it."

"Lisa—"

"No."

It was too much. I couldn't keep this up. His questions, his mysterious look, the mere presence of him. My desire for him. My lust for him. My fear of him. My fear of him and me together. I wasn't strong enough.

I was too broken. "You have to stop. You want to fix me—"

"No, I don't. I like you like this."

"What? Having a breakdown, standing in the fucking rain? You like this? You're a sick fucker."

He laughed. He fucking laughed at me. I was having a stage-three meltdown, and he was laughing.

I threw my arms up and spun away from him.

"You're the only one who can fix you," he hollered to my back. "All of the business stuff, though, you can figure that out. Just think about it. We all know you'll make it work."

I turned back around. "Why? Why do you think I can? I can't even figure out that a lighter doesn't work in the damn rain."

He laughed again. "You are so fucking hot."

"You are a disturbed individual."

He nodded, grinning at me.

And somehow, someway, his grin unclenched my body. It slowed my breathing and broke through my panic. I was shaky but no longer utterly overwhelmed.

How did he do it? How did he make me feel okay?

I slipped under the portico and stood in front of him, close enough for my chest to press into his abdomen. He dropped his arms. I cocked my head back to peer up at his light brown eyes, my favorite color. Flecks of green and gold shined at me.

"Don't give up, princess," he said and tucked a dripping lock of hair behind my ear.

"I love 'Uptown Girl'." It was always one of my favorites," I said in a soft voice I didn't recognize.

It almost sounded like I was eight years old again, clutching my Rainbow Dash doll when I was scared. She gave me comfort and confidence to stand up to the dentist or anything else I feared. Now I'm a grown-up with no security doll to hug, but there was Ben.

I backed away from him and stomped inside, straight to the ladies' room to clean myself up.

I yanked several paper towels from the dispenser and assessed the damage from my little act of insanity. My mascara had run down my cheeks like Courtney Love's album cover, a beauty queen with a tiara and a psychotic expression on her face.

While waiting for the water to warm up, my mind cleared. I took several long and deep breaths.

If we got an order from Kohl's with enough advance to pay off our debt to the Chinese manufacturer, then twelve-hundred pieces for Betty would be no problem. Except we couldn't sacrifice the headway we'd made to resurrect the brand's reputation.

Even though it only took two days for Jason to bring the Tennent name back from the dead, Betty would drop us, and the surf shops wouldn't touch us with a ten-foot pole if we appeared as "Tennent Surf Company" at another big discount retailer.

No, we needed a different name. A nom de plume like Shelly had for her books, but still Tennent's caché.

Ben was wearing one of our vintage TSC hats, and it hit me. Kohl's could have TSC as a label.

I swiped the wet paper towel across my cheeks, and a flutter started in my belly. TSC. That would work.

I threw my hair into a top knot and ran out of the bathroom, glancing at my watch at full gallop with my wet shoes sloshing. It was 2:36 PM—plenty of time.

"Brad," I shouted and stopped at the arm of the couch he was lounging on.

He stood and scanned me up and down. "What the hell, Lisa? You're soaked."

"Shut up and listen to me," I snapped, trying to catch my breath. Ben came up behind me. I pointed to his head. "How many TSC hats do we have?"

Brad walked over to a gray plastic bin in the corner, produced a stack of different colored, flat-billed caps, and counted.

"Six." He glanced back up at me.

"You didn't cancel the Kohl's meeting, did you?"

"No. I was waiting to see how long your freak out would last this time."

I sneered at him. Ben laughed, and I pointed at him and barked, "Don't."

He raised his hands in mock surrender.

I took the hats from Brad and called our team close. "Okay, here's the deal. Kohl's will get us as TSC, not Tennent, understood? We have to make it seem cool. So, everyone wears the hats—especially you, Jason. Ben, can you ask the deejay to do that 'Let's Dance' thing at exactly three-oh-five? When the buyer gets here?"

Shelly, Kelly, Brad, and Jason put their hats on, grinning at me.

"She's back, everyone," Jason cheered.

"Yeah." Brad pumped his fist like a dork. "I knew it, Lise. I knew you'd figure it out."

"Okay, don't get all confident yet. You've got to sell them and get a big ass contract today with enough advance to produce the jackets for Betty. Got it?"

"Got it." He nodded.

"An advance, Brad. It won't work without the advance. Tell them you have a meeting with Target at five o'clock or something.

That'll piss them off."

"Wait. Target's here?"

"No, Brad. Just no. Make this work. Just TSC. Right?" I reminded him to stay focused.

He gave me a thumbs up and went to the sample rack to adjust the garments. I took my hair tie off and put my hat on.

A group of young men came to the table, and Jason trotted over to sign posters for them. Shelly joined him, producing a marker from her pocket and proving how capable she was. They all showed me they were a great team.

Ben fetched more posters, and Kelly adjusted the printouts on the coffee tables.

I took some steps back, glanced at our banner, and could finally breathe regularly despite my heart beating so fast.

Ben glanced at me from the table with that look again. I couldn't read it for the life of me. Was it admiration? Fear? Jealousy? Hunger? Thirst?

This wasn't the time to try and figure it out.

# Chapter Nine

*Ben*

Lisa's number flashed on my phone. I was between my Uber rides, and it was close to ten-thirty the following Friday night after we'd gotten back from San Diego. That insane trip when she'd denied me her body and shut me out of her soul. I wasn't deterred. Not yet.

"Hey," I answered.

"Do you believe in God?" she slurred.

"Are you drunk?"

"No, I took an Ambien, then ate three chocolate-covered espresso beans, so I'm wired and buzzed, laying on the floor and thinking 'bout stuff."

"I think you're officially more fucked up than I am."

"That's good. I'm pretty competitive. I like winning." She sighed. "So? Do you?"

"Believe in God? Yes. She's probably pissed at you right now for abusing that spectacular body she gave you."

"She?"

"Yes, Lisa. God is a woman. She's got to be because only a woman could make the sea, the trees, the sky, and your fine ass—all of the beauty in the world. Also, men can't make humans, everyone knows that."

She didn't speak for a few moments, and I found myself parked outside her townhouse peering up at the second-floor windows behind white horizontal shutters.

"You've thought a lot about this," she grumbled.

"Eighteen months gives a guy a while to think."

Her window gave off a soft orange glow, and I imagined her lying on the floor, bathed in candlelight.

She was quiet for a few long, loud breaths.

"I'm not Rainbow Dash, you know. You are." She finally spoke with firm conviction in her voice. "The Dasher started selfish and arrogant, chasing the desire to belong to a group that wouldn't have her and making bad choices—"

"The Dasher?"

"Yeah, I called her The Dasher. Anyway, shut up and listen to my philosophy."

I chuckled. "A My Little Pony philosophy?"

"Yes. Okay, so, The Dasher realized the power of loyalty and friendship, and her powers grew. Then she could dash through time and space and help anyone, but her powers were no match for Nightmare Moon."

"I have no idea what you're talking about."

"Nightmare Moon was the evilest of evils." She paused then whispered, "I'm a nightmare."

"My favorite nightmare. One I don't want to wake up from."

"Don't be nice to me, Ben. I don't deserve it."

I shook my head even though she couldn't see me. "So, what happened to Nightmare Moon?"

A sound like she was taking a pull from a cigarette and blowing it out paused her speech. "The Dasher showed her the power of friendship and loyalty, and she turned back into Princess Luna." She then said in a soft voice, "Anyway, The Dasher saved the princess from herself. Episode five, Season one, Friendship is Magic." She was babbling sleepily.

I still had no idea what she was talking about. "Go to bed, princess."

"Wait. Are you driving tonight?"

"Yes."

After a minute, she said, "Be safe out there, Dasher."

"I will."

She hung up. I waited until her light went out.

Well, I guess I was going to have to go home and watch some *My Little Pony* to find out what in the fuck she was talking about.

My thoughts went to Chloe, and my heart hurt. I hadn't seen my baby girl in a few months after Marisol tried to get back together. I couldn't imagine being with a woman like her anymore. She was controlling and crazy jealous.

The night I'd left, she accused me of flirting with the computer network rep for her father's motorcycle shop. She came at me with a knife.

An actual knife, threatening to stab me for being unfaithful when she'd witnessed me bending over the computer woman showing me the new ordering software at the shop. I'd missed the group tutorial, and she'd offered to stay and teach me what the others had already learned.

I had to push Mari's knife-wielding crazy ass away from me. She fell over the couch side table, hitting her cheek on the coffee table. She used the bruise on her face to threaten me.

Even though I'd stayed and helped her with an icepack and was willing to talk, she wouldn't hear it and told me to leave. Then her father fired me. I stayed away, hoping everyone would cool off, but I missed Chloe.

It had been months, and I hadn't visited our three-year-old daughter, who loved My Little Pony.

I saw a vehicle request light up my phone and decided it would be my last for the night, and in the morning, I was going to text Marisol. I had to watch the show with my baby girl and find out why Lisa called me The Dasher.

*Episode five, Season one, Friendship is Magic.*

~ * ~

"I don't get how your new job works." Marisol took a bowl of unnatural, orange-tinged mac and cheese from the microwave and set it on Chole's highchair table.

I bent forward from my chair and blew on it. My big cheeked little sweetie blew on it, too, and giggled. I blew harder, and she mimicked me. Then I whistled into it, her eyes opened wide, and she tried to whistle, making a little spitting sound.

"I can't do it," her little helium voice complained.

"Yes, you can." I pointed to my mouth. "Now, pucker up, lower your bottom teeth without opening your mouth any more than this." I pointed to the small hole my mouth made. "Now blow slowly."

She did everything I told her, and a little toot came from her mouth. She smiled and made my whole body light up. Then she did it again and again. I joined the tooting along with her. She was dazzled by the sounds she was making, and I laughed at her delight.

"You did it, baby." I gave her a little peck on the lips. "You're amazing."

Marisol snorted. "Great. Now she won't eat and will make that noise for days."

"Oh, she'll get better. It just takes practice." I picked up her little fork. "Okay, whistle, then take a bite. Whistle, then take a bite." She did what I'd asked, making me puff my chest out in pride. I missed her so much.

Chloe was a determined character. She reminded me of my overachieving sister, with total focus on everything she did. Shelly was first in her high school class, then law school, and now a best-selling novelist. She was crazy in a different way than I was. Or Lisa was. For sure, a different crazy than Marisol was. Were all women a little crazy, or did I just not understand them?

"So, you're working for an old surfer as his assistant, like some Hollywood actor or something?"

I sat back in the chair of the kitchen table I'd bought for us when we moved into the apartment, and she'd hated it because it was square and not round.

"Exactly," I answered. "Jason's styling a clothing line and starting a surf school for underprivileged kids, so he hired me to help."

"Underprivileged? Like poor Hispanics? Like my family?"

She had accused me many times of being biased toward her Latino family even though they were sixth-generation Americans, her father had a successful business, and she'd grown up in a big house in Lakewood.

"Your family isn't poor."

She put her hand on her hip and sneered at me. "Maybe not my immediate family, but aunts, uncles, cousins—they are what you white man would call 'underprivileged.'"

"Well, then send them to us to learn how to surf," I snarked.

She huffed and turned back to the dishes. Now I felt terrible. She had a way of making me feel guilty for being white and 'privileged.' Yeah, me. The son of an elevator salesman.

"Are you still going out?"

"Yes, I've got to get dressed." She peered at the clock above the stove and threw her dishtowel on the counter. Then she glared at me with concern. "Will you stay with her? I don't know how late I will be."

"Of course. She's my daughter. I miss her." I took a noodle from Chloe's plate and popped it into my mouth, and she giggled.

"Hey, Daddy. Mine."

"What? No, mine." I took another noodle and teased her by holding it to my mouth but not eating it.

She picked up two noodles and held them out to me. "Eat more."

She was such a sweet girl—all rainbows and sunshine.

"We're going to watch hours and hours of *My Little Pony*. And eat ice cream. Right, Pinkie-Pie?" I said to Chloe.

"No, I'm Apple Jack, the cowgirl pony," she snapped at me.

"Oh, I don't know Apple Jack." I scooped up another forkful for her. "My friend calls me The Dasher."

"Rainbow Dash?" Chloe asked with her eyes as wide as dinner plates.

I nodded.

My baby girl clapped. "Daddy Dasher."

She liked that name, repeating it several times in a sing-song. I didn't think my heart could expand any more than it had.

"Okay, her bedtime is seven o'clock. Two books—then sit with her until she falls asleep. The rocker is still next to the bed," Mari said.

I nodded, remembering all the times I sat with Chloe in that rocker, feeding her a bottle and reading her little books. Everything in my world changed when she entered it, and I couldn't waste another minute away from her. But I didn't want to be with her mother. I preferred the blonde debutante princess who was crazier than I was.

Shelly told me that Lisa had confided in her about her troubles getting pregnant and how she'd decided to have a hysterectomy to make it final. I wondered how she would be around Chloe. If she even liked kids or if she just thought she should have them because she was married back then and settled and getting older.

I wished she'd talk to me about real things, not just work, cartoon characters, or how she'd thought men were useless.

*Patience, man. She's got to get herself right first.*

# Chapter Ten

*Lisa*

Necessity was the mother of invention. I heard the phrase often enough. Desperation could also make a person think hard and long about any solution. I was desperate for one.

Hence my mind went to Mark Carpenter, a funny guy with a self-deprecating sense of humor and a touch of sarcasm that I dug. He was from Minneapolis, had a polite, mid-western thing, and asked me on a proper date after talking a few times.

He ran a hedge fund company, and I hoped he could help me find extra funding without taking on a partner or mansplaining investors. Was it cool to talk business on a date? I hadn't been on one in almost fifteen years.

I finished applying my makeup. Mark was picking me up in just a few hours, and I primed myself to look my successful best, someone he could advise. We had to hire more warehouse staff and pay for production in China. That meant cash. I also tried to appear attractive enough if anything else came of this date.

Mentally, I ran through how I would pitch it. Even though it was important, try as I might, I couldn't focus on my meeting with Mark. Thoughts of Ben kept interjecting.

Images of his face. His hands. His lips. His kisses—of how much he still liked me, and I knew he liked me a ton.

But I couldn't be with him. He was from a different world. I couldn't date him; he'd hate my lifestyle, and I wouldn't subject him to the scrutiny of small minds. He'd be chirped about if I brought him to any social events with his tattoos, and God forbid anyone found out about his jail time or illegitimate child.

Since January, he was always at the warehouse. We'd become default partners-in-design and because he worked for Jason, and apparently for me, I'd come to rely on his opinions. He was talented and attentive to the minor details, from where zippers would be placed to the fabrics that were best for each garment. He had expensive taste, and although I would have loved to use some of the pieces he'd suggested, it would bring the cost up too much on the garments' production.

He was sexy and had a sense of style but had no college education or financial stability.

*Oh, fuck me and my fucked-up head.*

I'd thought my head was finally getting to a much better place. Then rumblings of a county-wide shutdown from the Covid Pandemic started. I wouldn't let myself get anxious about it. Yet.

However, the pandemic was taking over, and by early March, the TVs everywhere were on constantly with updates of when everything would shut down. Our spring shipment was weeks late, and Brad had been pleading with Betty to be patient. We couldn't screw her over now that she'd taken a chance on us.

Focused on finishing our summer line with Ben, due to show the stores by the end of the month, I was calmer than I thought I'd be. Working through all of the noise was the perfect distraction.

I didn't tell him about my date with Mark. Ben might be the violent, jealous type. I had no idea. We didn't have anything between us besides work, even after the night he gave me his body because he knew I needed it. He kept his distance after I denied his advances in San Diego. We just focused on our task of the summer line for Tennent.

One night, he watched me steam press a pair of board shorts then asked to try it. I loved having a partner to share the designing with, a fresh perspective, and a male one at that. Dottie was stuck in the old designs, but he was an opinionated breath of fresh air, even though we'd argue sometimes. He'd relent to my experience, and I'd accept his style aesthetic as our target market. We made a great team.

I'd catch him staring at me with those multicolored eyes, light brown, gold, and green. On occasion, they'd darken, almost black, telling me he was aroused. I'd caught myself quite a few times remembering our night together, and my body heated up. The staring contests didn't last long. Either someone would come into the room, or I'd pull away.

~ * ~

Mark was picking me up at seven-thirty, and I'd gone through six different outfit combinations. Thankfully, I knew where we were going and the image I'd decided to portray to him, more confident than sexy, but a little sexy. I'd decided on leather leggings, a lace top, and a burgundy blazer.

Now for the shoes. I stared at my shoe closet for something that didn't come across like I was trying to be too young but not too old. Also, I was five-foot-eight and didn't know how tall he was. I didn't want to tower over him like my friend, Sandra, did with her husband, Kevin.

He'd gotten a complex with her in heels, and she had to get rid of her gorgeous shoes. Too bad she was a size seven and, therefore, too small for me to inherit her treasures. I would have liked her burgundy Gucci Mary-Janes right now.

I settled on my Prada ankle boots, not too high and well broken in.

My phone lit up with a call. Probably Mark. When I glanced at the caller ID, it was Shelly. My brows wrinkled in confusion. "Hi, Shelly. How are you?"

"Hey, Lisa. Do you have a minute?"

I sat on the white velvet stool at my vanity in the bathroom—my stomach dove and twisted; she sounded concerned. "Sure."

She sighed. "I know Ben has been at the warehouse a lot lately, and you two are getting close. I was wondering if you could talk to him for me?"

My curiosity peaked, but then a tingle of nerves chilled my neck. Had she known about my night with Ben last December after her wedding?

"I'm just going to come out with it. I don't hold back anymore, you know? Life's too damn short to worry about being the concierge of proprieties."

*Concierge of proprieties?* No wonder her fans loved her so much. She had a way with words.

Now that I knew Shelly wasn't going to ask me about my sex life with her brother—or lack thereof—I relaxed a bit. I checked my lipstick in my lit mirror and replied, "Of course. What's up?"

"I haven't seen my niece since she was born. Ben keeps putting me off like I'm going to corrupt the kid or something. I don't know. So, will you talk with him? You know, suggest a visit down here? The two of you and Chloe? Like a beach day or something? Maybe for surfing? Jason would love that."

I felt attacked or called out like she knew something was between Ben and me. "I don't know, Shelly."

"It's just… Sorry to ask, but he seems to listen to you."

My head fell back, and I took a deep breath. I didn't have a unique way with him or anything. We worked well together, that was it.

He was crushing on me, but that was as far as it would go. Being around a kid wasn't something I needed in my life right now. I didn't like kids. No maternal desire to have them or be around them. Nope, if I did talk to him, I wouldn't go. I was going to keep my distance.

Should I even get involved with their family stuff? "I don't think he'll listen to me."

"Oh, he will. He—he *values* your friendship. He thinks of me as another parent because we are eleven years apart. Not a friend with any influence. Pleeeeeease," she begged, then giggled.

"I thought you were a lawyer, Shelly. Since when do lawyers beg?"

"It's a secret tactic but only used out of desperation. Please, pretty please? Please, please, please?"

"Ugh, fine," I said with a smile. "You are persuasive, counselor."

"You'll come too?"

I sighed. "I'm not good around kids."

"I'll have alcohol." She chuckled. "Please, Lisa, I should know my niece. I have all men in my life, and I haven't been able to give my expert feminine advice to anyone. I'd love to have a relationship with her."

That made me think of Mom and how Brad wouldn't have been able to live with her through her hip surgery recovery. It was on me to take care of her, bathe and dress her. I remember her brief talk about my body changing in adolescence in a rare moment of attention I'd craved.

She'd comforted me when my inability to have children broke me, and even though she said she'd supported my decision to leave David, I was still skeptical.

She'd been the feminine voice I'd needed at the time. "Okay, Shelly, I'll talk to him tomorrow."

"Yes. Thank you. I promise to have enough mimosas to make any kid tolerable."

My phone buzzed with a message from my Ring front porch camera. The image of a dark-haired man in a sports jacket and white-collared shirt appeared. Mark. "Gotta go. I will try, Shelly."

"That's all I can ask. Goodnight, Lisa."

I tugged my boots on, then ran downstairs. Thank goodness Maria had been over earlier to clean. I wasn't the best housekeeper and didn't want Prince Charming to think I was a slob.

I opened the door to a dazzling white smile.

"Wow, you're prettier in person," he said, and my body warmed.

Mark Carpenter was the kind of man I should be with: educated, cultured, and from a good family. He took my hand and kissed it. "Shall we? We have reservations at Nobu in Newport."

An imperial smile formed on his lips like I was supposed to gasp with sheer delight or something. I wasn't as blown away as he expected me to be with the very expensive restaurant choice. Mom had many events there over the years with her charities and we knew the chef and management very well.

Still, I mustered a smile. We strolled to his car together. He lifted the gull-wing door of his Tesla open for me, and I almost fell into the seat. I let out a little giggle as the door glided closed. He circled the other side, not noticing my purse strap caught in the door. I tried to find the handle, and when he opened his door, I showed him the problem by tugging on my purse.

"Oh, it's uh-there." He pointed, and I lifted some almost camouflaged handle, cracked the door, then slammed it back down. His face screwed up in a cringe. "It has a sensor. You don't have to slam it."

"Oh, sorry."

"It's brand new, and it's not like our tough Detroit-made cars. I feel like if I breathe on it wrong, it's going to fall apart." He settled in and pushed a button. No sound came, just a low hum and a lit dashboard to let you know the power was on.

Electric cars freaked me out sometimes with their silent mode.

He had *Bloomberg News* on satellite radio and let it play instead of talking to me.

Awkward. Not the mood I thought this evening would have. There was still time to try and change it, though.

"So, how long have you been in California?" I almost had to shout.

"About four years. There's a lot of Biotech here, and we're going to concentrate on that."

I nodded with nothing to add. I didn't know anything about Biotech. He talked about it for ten minutes before switching his diatribe to investments, manufacturers, and finally, shipping costs and supply chain issues.

*Ah, now he is speaking my language.*

I interrupted his babbling and said, "Yes, we have a shipment that hasn't even left Beijing yet. It's been delayed for four months, and we were supposed to receive and process it by the end of this month. It's a mess."

He glanced at me like I was an alien. "You get a lawyer and sue them."

I sighed. "It's not that simple."

Brad had talked to Shelly about our options. A lawsuit would take too long and cost too much money. She'd been in the import business before she retired to write full-time, and she'd advised against it.

But more than that, it became apparent that Mark was the last person to take advice from regarding business relationships. He was a money vulture who'd swoop in and buy carcasses of companies, invest the bare minimum of capital to make it attractive, then sell the business off without setting foot in the door or getting to know the people. I knew all about it. My ex-husband was a board member of two such investment companies. It was a heartless business, just like my ex-husband.

We pulled up to the valet at the stunning marina-side restaurant. I had been there plenty of times but was always enamored of the gorgeous location. The bobbing boats and twinkling lights in the marina framed by the darkening purple sunset on the horizon were ethereal and calming.

We were taken to the second-floor balcony and seated along the railing. Smiling, Mark towed my chair out.

"You are better than my aunt described," he commented as he sat.

The hostess grinned at me and winked when she handed me the menu. He was a charmer.

"Thank you," I said, not knowing if he meant my looks or my personality, although he hadn't asked anything about me to make any assessment of my personality.

I knew what to order and usually preferred to sit with the sushi chefs at the bar, chatting with them about what was fresh. They'd always reserved some secret catch for customers who requested *Omakase* or 'chef's choice.' The experience was different at a table. The view was terrific, and the heat lamp kept me warm.

He ordered a passible sake, not the best, however. I didn't say anything about his choice. When he started talking about his business again, I tried to seem interested.

He told me about his move to California, house hunting, business partners, and summer vacation in Tuscany for his sister's wedding.

I'd poured and sipped my sake several times. I'd started doing shots by the time he told me about his ex-wife and his expectations of the woman who would become his next wife.

"I want three kids right away, boom, boom, boom." He snapped his fingers. "I'm not getting any younger and already have a five-bedroom house and a Labradoodle. So, all that's missing is a wife." He leaned in on his elbows. "How about you?"

His whispered question made my spicy salmon start coming back up my throat. It was as if the question would entice me when really, it just made me sick. Or maybe it was all the alcohol I drank.

"Uh, I guess your Aunt Carolyn didn't tell you, but I can't have kids." I picked up my napkin and held it to my lips to ensure it would be discreet if I did wretch.

"Oh, no, she didn't tell me." He sat back.

"Yup," I quipped. God, I was drunk. "It's all gone now. Not that it *ever* worked." I waved my hand above my lap.

"Really? Didn't you try drugs or surgery? Or insemination or any of that?"

His questions were making my blood boil.

"Of course, we tried. We tried everything." I was a bit loud, and a few patrons turned toward our table. Tears were building. I couldn't relive any of my plunges into darkness or justify my efforts to Mr. Talks-About-Himself.

*"Keep her pregnant and subservient."* That was the trajectory of my life with him, and every other guy like him. He was just as bad as my ex.

"I didn't mean to upset you," he said, but his eyes showed no empathy, simply disappointment.

"I need the restroom." I rose.

He stood with me as his proper upbringing told him to do, but his eyes were flat. He didn't care about me or if I'd make it across the room. No, he was—*assessing* me—like I was a challenging business negotiation, and he had to recalculate.

I gave him a little smirk, and my chest constricted. As I marched to the bathroom, I opened my Uber app. It was a chicken-shit thing to do, but I was leaving. I couldn't endure another second of this guy's *boom, boom, boom,* and Labradoodle. If I had to deal with the wrath and scorn of Mom's friends, then so be it.

I glanced over my shoulder to make sure I had a clear path down the stairs and out to the valet. My phone buzzed.

*Driver: Benjamin: White Toyota, Camry license plate GVT806, two minutes.*

I hit 'accept' and stopped at the end of the driveway, trying to exhale my anger only to find myself muttering curse words and pacing like a caged panther.

A white sedan stopped, the driver's door flew open, and he ran to me, throwing his arms around my shoulders and drawing me into his leather and citrus-scented wall of a chest. The sight of him was pure relief. My tears finally fell. I cried with great big sobs. Ben. *The Dasher* rescued me. Again.

"Hey, hey," he said, cradling my head back to look at my face. "Bad date?" he joked.

The gold in his eyes flashed, and I stepped back. He was wearing a tight white T-shirt and a flat-billed hat backward.

"How are you here?" I wiped my eyes.

"I was down the street and ready to quit for the night. When I saw your name, I—"

"Let's go," I snapped and pushed away from him.

I didn't mean to. Just like every time, he elicited so many emotions inside me. I missed him, but I didn't. I had to have him, but I couldn't. He was so good to me and breaking down my walls.

He was everything I'd needed and nothing I'd wanted.

I got in the back. He didn't say a word.

I sniffed and reached to take a tissue from the pocket on the back of the seat. Before he could speak, I told him not to ask me about it.

"Okay," he said. I caught his eye in the rearview mirror. "So, straight home, or should I find you something to pound with a rubber mallet? We could stop by the warehouse, and you could take it out on the design table."

I scoffed. That did sound like a great idea.

"I know of a boxing gym not too far from here. Maybe they have some guy you could spar with or just stand there and let you punch him. I'm sure he'd allow it if you paid him enough."

That sounded excellent too.

I shook my head and dabbed my eyes with the tissue. "Just home."

"Do you need anything? Ice cream? A donut? Some *Ambien* and espresso beans?"

He was something else, something not of my world of men who try to fix me, who tell me what I should want and explain why I should listen to them. No, Ben just wished me to be happy. His suggestions were also band-aids. Not a solution for my many issues.

He stopped in front of my house, put the car in park, and turned around to address me in the back seat. When he stretched his forearm across the back of the passenger seat, the tattooed rainbow colors on his skin reminded me how different he was from Mark.

"I've noticed that you get clarity when you take the time to think. Even standing in a rainstorm."

I snorted. "A long hot bath would be better." I was serious. Band-aids help you not bleed all over everything, and a My Little Pony bandage always made me feel better.

"Do it. I'm here if you're ready to talk."

I shook my head. Why was he so sweet to me? "Thanks, I'll be okay. Maybe no dating for a while."

"Just sex?" His face flushed, and the corner of his dark pink lip curved up.

"I've got vibrator-of-the-month, thanks," I said.

He took a deep breath. "A waterproof one?"

I laughed. "Yeah, but that's not where my head is."

"Maybe it should be. Want some sexting to assist you? I'm kind of a master at it."

I considered that for a second. "Really?"

"Yeah, my sister isn't the only one in my family who's good with words. I'm a brilliant wordsmith. When it comes to dirty talk anyway."

My face heated. God, I was considering this. "I'll think about it. Thank you again for the ride, Ben."

"It's my job. Well, one of them." He chuckled.

"Are you coming to the warehouse tomorrow?" I asked.

"Yeah. Around eleven to pick up those permits for Jason."

Right, Jason was starting a surf school for underprivileged kids. Brad had gotten him the forms to sign.

"Okay." I stopped halfway out the door. "See you tomorrow, Ben."

"Hey, Lisa? Will you call me The Dasher again? I liked it."

I laughed but didn't answer him. I was so high when I told him he was Rainbow Dash saving Nightmare Moon.

"Sleep well, princess," he said.

I closed the door. He waited for me to get inside, then his headlights beamed through the front window as he drove away.

He was The Dasher. Maybe someday he would turn me into Princess Luna and not the nightmare I was. In what world would that work for us? A bird could love a fish, but where would they live? Drew Barrymore said that.

# Chapter Eleven

*Huntington Beach, CA*
*Ben*

"You're so smart," Mom cheered Chloe. "That's right, baby."

The two of them were working on one of Mom's projects, where she took broken pottery and glued the pieces together with gold to show the seams. She said she liked flaws and gave me a knowing glance when she explained it to my daughter.

Mom always understood me. "Say, Kintsugi."

"Kishhhhuugii," Chloe slurred.

"That's my brilliant girl." She hugged her granddaughter.

Mom had retired from being an elementary school nurse to take care of Dad full-time since he'd been battling Alzheimer's. She kept begging me to bring Chloe over. The disease was bringing out the crazy conspiracy side of Dad's personality, or maybe it was a side effect of watching too much Fox News on their TV night and day. I assumed she needed some granddaughter time to lighten up the house.

As soon as we walked in the door, my father shouted from one of the back bedrooms. "Is that Sam? Sam, come'ere. I want to show you something."

Sam was Dad's older brother who died in Vietnam in 1972. I guess I resembled him sans the tattoos.

I gazed at Mom, and my blood pressure shot up. It wasn't the first time he'd confused me with a dead man, but it still made me uncomfortable to be around him.

Mom urged me to go, making shooing motions with her hands. I wasn't sure about playing this game with him. His delusional episodes could get frightening. I scrubbed my hand over my mouth and conjured a thread of empathy for the man who'd pushed me too far too many times before the illness. Now, I was supposed to play Uncle Sam, the revered, respectable soldier who'd been dead for fifty years.

The hallway hadn't changed in all that time either. Yellowing, browning collages of family photos taken with Kodak cameras over the years lined the walls. Never changing.

Photos of Dad's family at the beach in the 1950s and 60s, where he looked just like my nephew Connor with light blond hair, tan, tall, and lean with small shoulder muscles like the baseball player he was. Like Connor, a real jock. Not like me.

My mom, in her flowing hippie dresses, mirrored Shelly, with long dark blonde mermaid hair and a sparkling smile. Their wedding photo was taken in a studio with a fake marble background and posed like a prom photo. Forced and formal, how Dad liked it.

I always imagined how Mom was earthy back then—dancing barefoot like a flower child at concerts, doing her pottery, drinking tea, and philosophizing. At the same time, he was structured, corporate, serious, and boring. I couldn't understand how the two of them got together being such opposites.

She told me the story every time I'd asked. And I asked many times because I was still trying to figure out what she saw in him.

*"Your father had a good job and bought me a house in a nice neighborhood and a car. My own car. Back then, that was a big deal. I was tired of dating men who craved to be free of responsibilities, doing drugs, and refusing to work for a living. One even asked me to live in a commune and be the fourth of his three wives he'd already had." She giggled and rolled her eyes. "Your father and I balanced each other. He relaxed with me. Well, a little." She shrugged. "But I needed structure too. I wanted to be a nurse, and he paid for my school. We love each other's quirks. It's balanced us both."*

"Ah, Sam." Dad glanced up from a cardboard box and motioned for me to enter the bedroom.

"Hey, Da-uh-Roger," I stuttered.

He motioned to my tattoos. "What did you do to your arms? Is that some kind of new skin treatment?"

Uncle Sam had chronic eczema and tried different things he'd read about to cure it. Dad meant my tattoos.

"Uh, yeah. A new treatment." I rubbed my arm, insecure about the blobs of color that had been redone so many times there were no real images, just blurred-out reminders of my past bad decisions.

"Look at this." He held up a metal toy car about the size of his thumb. "My Matchbox Chevy Belaire." He said gazing at it. "Or was this one yours?"

He and his brother were just twelve months apart and were raised just like twins. They were almost identical in all the photos—same hair and smiles. They dressed alike and received the same gifts for birthdays and Christmas.

"I forget," I said, sitting beside him on the bed.

The moment allowed me to study him—full head of white-gray hair and creases in the corners of his light brown eyes.

I decided to be Sam because Dad's soft, sweet expression was never given to me. Perpetual anger and disappointment shone in his eyes for me. "Wasn't mine red?"

Dad pursed his lips and focused on the toy. "Was it?"

He finally glanced at me and furrowed his brows. The realization was slow, but the change was instant. His body stiffened, and the expression on his face changed, hardened with that same disappointment and resentment.

He spat, "Take your hat off inside the house, boy."

I yanked my navy TSC hat off and ran a hand over my hair. Even the strands were frustrating. Another tender moment with him, however unreal, was over.

"Sorry, sir." I jerked back at his scowl.

"Well? Did you get a job?" he snapped and stood with the box.

"I did. I'm working with Jason, Shelly's husband."

He shook his head, and his face changed again. "Jason? No, no, Shelly's married to Eric, the guy from Chicago. The Cubs fan."

I wasn't about to explain that Eric had died five years ago, and she remarried the surf legend. Dad was at the wedding, after all.

I needed a change in conversation. "I brought Chloe. She's in the kitchen with Mom. Come see her."

"Chloe?" He grumbled but went into the hallway. "Who in the hell is Chloe?"

My heart skipped and dropped. I followed him, keeping a distance behind him and trying to calm myself from exploding from his lack of empathy for me.

The third time Dad called Chloe "Shelly," Mom told him to go lay down.

Chloe had gold paint all over her hands and arms and some on her chubby cheek.

"She does remind me of your sister," Mom confessed when he was out of earshot. "What do they call it? Obsessive Compulsive Disorder?"

I laughed. "You think Shelly's OCD too?"

"Maybe." She dabbed her paintbrush onto the teapot. "But it seemed to work for her even though I can't read that filthy book of hers." She shuddered dramatically. "Too much sex."

Everything Shelly did was perfect. I hated and admired her for it when we were growing up. Now I just admired the hell out of her.

I went into the kitchen, unraveled a few paper towels, and wet them. Mom's kitchen was spotless, as always, and Shelly was the same way. I probably was too. I liked things in their place. We were a family of neat freaks. Then there was Lisa. She was messy. Gorgeous and sexy, but messy, and I loved figuring her out.

"So," Mom said as I returned, "tell me about Lisa Tennent. You've been working for the woman for a while. Are you going to tell me anything about her?"

"Nothing to tell."

"Aww, come on. All I have is your father's crazy theories about being monitored by Microsoft through the water supply. Are you attracted to her?"

"I'm not discussing this with you, Mom. There's nothing to tell." I handed her the wet paper towels, and she wiped Chole's cheek.

The three-year-old didn't move or flinch from her task of finding the pieces that went together and glopped enough gold paint on the seams to seal a dam.

"There's got to be something. You two left together after the wedding." Mom's eyebrow raised, even though she didn't glance at me.

I hadn't realized how obvious we were that night.

"She's dealing with a lot, and she doesn't need my shit. That's it." I sat and watched Chloe.

Mom sat up straight as a mannequin and glared at me. "Such vile language, and what *stuff*? You are working, and you've been great with Chloe. You're being responsible."

"My uh…stuff isn't that far enough in the past to be forgotten. She only knows half of it." I picked up a paintbrush and made the outline of a horse in gold paint on the flattened-out paper bag used to line the table, and before I knew it, I was painting a gold Rainbow Dash. When I looked up, they stared at me with the same eyes and expressions.

"The Dasher." Chloe pointed. "That's you, Daddy. Cause you're a rainbow." She pointed to my arms.

Mom's hand flew to her mouth, and tears formed in her eyes. "That's so beautiful. You're right, Chloe. Your daddy is a rainbow."

"Daddy's friend calls him that," Chloe announced and returned to her task.

"Who? Lisa?" Mom's eyes opened wide. She met my gaze, and I inwardly groaned. No escaping the topic now.

I said, quite against my will, "She thinks I'm like Rainbow Dash because I'm her…friend."

Mom's lips pursed like she was holding a damn soliloquy inside. *Shit.* "Help me in the kitchen. Now."

It was an order. I stood, and so did she. After a kiss on Chloe's forehead, Mom marched into the kitchen. I followed her. She threw the paper towels in the trash under the sink, straightened up with a sigh, and placed her hand on her hips. Her glare was ferocious.

"What's going on?" She leaned her hip against the counter.

"She's South County money, Ma. Her life is social stuff and charity things, and she was a debutante and had a *coat-illian* thing with white gloves and s…stuff. I can't live in that world, not with this." I waved my hands over my inked forearms. "And my past." I leaned on the opposite counter and exhaled. "She can't have kids, and I don't think she likes them either. How am I supposed to be with someone who won't be around my daughter?"

"That's ridiculous. If she wants to be with you, she'll have to take all of you. Just the way you are."

"That's the thing. I'm changing. Being around Jason has made me more chilled. He's given me some clarity, and I'm embracing my art more."

"I'm so glad to hear that. You know, Dad and I fought about that constantly. I begged him to send you to art school before you got in trouble. Darn it all." She almost cursed, hanging her head and shaking it. "I should have pushed back more. Maybe you wouldn't have had so much—"

Her hand flew up to her eyes, and she sobbed, then slammed a fist on the counter. Not once had I seen her this angry.

"I was taught to listen to my husband, no matter what, or he'd leave me, and I wouldn't be able to survive." She rolled her eyes through her tears. "What a load of crock."

"Mom, just say 'shit' for once in your life. He won't fucking remember tomorrow anyway."

She wiped her eyes, then stared at me with conviction. "You can still go to art school. Get a degree."

I gently took her hands in mine. Mom was the most empathetic person I'd ever known. She truly felt others' emotions. It broke my heart to think of all the feelings she had to suppress over the years.

"I'm doing my art with Lisa. It's fine. I'm helping her design the clothing line for Jason. It's one of the things that's making me feel right, for once."

"What about her?" Mom glared at me. It was shrewd and understanding like she could see things I couldn't. "Does she love you?"

The question sent chills through me. How could my mother see what was happening to me where Lisa was concerned? Was that what mothers did? Did they just know stuff about you and how you felt about a particular debutante?

"I'm— She needs time to figure her stuff out. I made a deal with myself to be patient but stay in her vicinity, so she won't forget about me."

"What does she need to figure out?"

"What she wants, and who she's going to be? Maybe a mid-life crisis? I don't know. For now, she has to save her father's company since he took off. It's all on her. I'm trying to help but not get in her way."

"Oh, pshaw." Mom pushed my arm. "Get in her way, Benny. Let her know every day how much you like her, even through her crisis. Give her confidence. Make her feel attractive and desired. That's what we all crave as we get older. She probably feels less of a woman since she can't have children. Your Aunt Elise was the same way. Uncle Stan was there for her every day, making sure she felt good about herself until the day she died. His dedication was inspiring. Now I'm there for Dad, ensuring he feels like a human even if his brain is going haywire. It's what we do for the people we love."

I nodded, and we both jumped when a crash came from the dining room. We ran in to find Chloe in front of a pile of ceramic pieces.

"It's okay," Chloe said, her hands out to stop us from advancing. "We Kinstuggie, again."

She was the most confident toddler.

Mom turned to me. "I love her so much."

I was truly lucky to have great women in my life but the infinite guilt over my younger, angry years was eating me alive. It had less to do with Mom and more with Dad and his 1950s TV-Dad view of family, and I hated it. He was the man. He made the money, paid the bills, and alone decided how life would be.

I craved more. I liked expensive things and shortcuts, some danger, and a lot of passion. To Dad, boys played sports and worked an honest but boring as hell job, working their way up a management ladder wearing short sleeve buttoned shirts and ugly polyester ties, just like him and his father and his father before him.

Shelly told me to read Jack Kerouac when I was in high school. I didn't because I didn't do anything my sister told me to do. Although I did read it in jail, and it spoke to me. I ended up reading all of his books and his contemporaries. I had to buy a motorcycle when I got out. I was going to be the opposite of what my father expected. I suppose I took things a bit too far in my rebellion. I was good at being bad.

"See." Mom held up a beautiful teapot with veins of gold threaded through it.

With the flaws running through the delicate porcelain, the pot's current state was so much more beautiful. "Can I have that one?"

"Of course." She handed it to me. "Are you drinking tea these days?"

"No, but I know someone who does."

"Ahh, your debutante, eh?"

"Yeah," I said and held it up to examine every side of it with its baby blue and gold perfection. This teapot was Lisa and her beautiful imperfections.

Mom was right. I would 'get in her way' and show her how my friendship and loyalty would win her over. I couldn't think of anything else. Lisa was it for me. For the first time, there was no shortcut. I'd have to wait for her to give in.

# Chapter Twelve



*Lisa*

"Well, you've put a cute little patch on the hole in your sinking ship," Uncle Steve announced, his smug and infuriating face on the computer screen. He insisted on a Zoom call with the lockdown in effect.

All I could see was the scene behind him overlooking the Balboa Bay Club marina, knowing his sixty-foot boat was somewhere out there, and Tennent had helped him buy it.

I explained it to him at the start of the conversation—all about the waiting, the shipments, the delays, and everything else. He seemed to take joy in the problems as if it was proof that I couldn't handle it.

Which annoyed the shit out of me.

I gave him my most saccharine smile. "I got a pallet of Hello Kitty patches in bulk from Costco delivered yesterday."

He ignored my sarcasm. "Do you have a plan yet, Lisa?"

"Nope," I replied nonchalantly. "I also hired the Titanic band and purchased life preservers."

"If the joking is finished, I'd like to have a real conversation." He glared at me as I spewed caustic words.

I meant them as a joke, but as they floated in the air, I realized I was talking like the woman before the Triple S Show who had an epiphany in the pouring rain and made it work. My team supported me in a display of loyalty led by Ben I didn't know if I'd ever be able to appreciate fully.

Things were different now. Ben was a big reason why. That damn tattooed ex-con was the best friend I'd ever had. The only one who'd believed in me from the beginning and didn't let me fall over the edge.

He'd shown up to the warehouse every day since the lockdown, threw the trash out, fixed scuffs in the walls, counted the hangers, and rearranged the storerooms.

He drew, sketched and created a series of cartoons with the Reaper surfer, which were dark, funny, and cool as shit, taking our blackest days and making them ironic.

We had images for five seasons of T-shirts. Brad sent emails and posted on our social media instead of making his road trip to the stores. No orders yet. Betty's finished jackets were on a container ship that hadn't left China and was terribly late for a September delivery to the stores.

"The bank isn't on hold just because you want it to be." Steve fiddled with his phone.

"Jason's wife is trying to get our goods released, and we've sent requests for extensions to the vendors, but, no, I don't have a plan."

"All right, keep treading water. Lisa, you need to figure out what happens next. I know some parties who would be interested in purchasing the assets."

I shook my head. Not in my lifetime would anyone own this company but a Tennent.

~ * ~

It was close to nine AM, and I had just arrived for another futile workday. Jason's truck was parked outside the warehouse, and Ben would be inside.

As soon as I walked in, I smelled him, and tingles shot down my spine. As much as I pushed him away, he'd remained steady as a rock. We discussed designs, and I taught him how to make the clothes he envisioned. His sketches were becoming more and more detailed and better than some of my classmates at Parsons. He refused to learn how to sew until I threatened him that I wouldn't make samples of his designs anymore until he learned.

We argued over fabrics and shared long, desperate, lingering stares. There were so many times I had to stop myself from wrapping my arms around him from the back when he was leaning over the design table, cutting patterns, or making swatch boards.

"Can you take me to L.A.? This afternoon? I need Jason's truck to pick up the bolts of fabric in Vernon." I asked.

He glanced up from the sewing machine he'd been cursing at. His fingers were caught in a web of thread and a needle stuck between his teeth. His perpetual flat, billed hat was on backward. His pink flushed cheeks showed his frustration, and it was adorable.

"What in the hell do I do now?" he barked and held up his imprisoned fingers.

I chuckled. "Free yourself, toss the bobbin, get a new one, and start again."

"I'm never going to figure this shit out. How 'bout we make a deal? You sew, and I'll cut. You can't stay in the lines anyway, and you hate cutting."

I held up my expensive scissors and motioned to cut the air. "I'll think about it."

"Do not ever make the cutting motion to a man." He winced.

I rolled my eyes. "So, yes? You'll take me this afternoon?"

He threw the ball of wasted thread into the trash next to the machine and stood. "Just us? All afternoon?" He closed the distance between us, making me tingly.

"There's a place I'd love to take you if it's open." I cocked my head back to meet him in the eye.

This little flirtatious dance was a regular thing when we were alone, but it didn't go further than sharing a breath's distance from each other without touching. Touching would progress into more. He was a mountain of restraint, and I was weakening.

"Oh, yeah? What kind of place do you want to show me?" His gaze went to my chest.

I was wearing a ribbed tank top under an open cardigan. He could glimpse down the low neckline, and a little growl came from his throat. The thought of pressing my breasts against his body flashed through my mind and stayed there. God, it would feel good. So so good.

I was still toying with the idea when he cleared his throat, stepped away, and adjusted the crotch of his shorts.

I smirked and retrieved my purse. "Let's go now," I declared and shouted to Brad that we were picking up more fabric.

"Lead the way." Ben bowed.

After two hours of '90s punk on the sound system, we drove up to Buffalo Exchange in Hollywood. Ben turned the enormous pickup into the empty parking lot of the turquoise building.

"Surprise," I sang. "Have you ever heard of this place?"

"No, should I have?" he asked.

"Oh, Ben." I shook my head. "A vintage shopper like you has never heard of Buffalo Exchange?"

"Vintage?"

"Yup. This place is legendary," I said.

The smell of old leather and Grandma's attic hit us as soon as we walked in.

"Welcome to Buffalo Exchange," a husky but perky male voice called from the glass counter to the left of us wearing a tie-dyed facemask.

The glow on Ben's face was like the sun peeking through the clouds. He seemed to be jumping inside like a little boy at the ice cream store, and the gold flecks in his eyes shone in the exposed fluorescent lights. We put our facemasks on and went in farther, taking in the rounders of multicolored garments well-organized for a vintage shop or thrift store.

"You got Doc Marten's?" he asked the long-haired guy with a brown flannel behind the counter, who seemed to be invoking Kurt Cobain's style.

"Shit, yeah, man. Back here." He walked toward the back of the store.

Ben went to follow him but got distracted by a green cargo jacket. He whispered to me, "Dolce and Gabbana knock off." Then he let the sleeve go.

I didn't ask how he knew that.

His eyes widened at the wall of clunky work boots in all colors and patterns.

"What size are the 1460 Vonda's?" He pointed to a black pair with red embroidered roses.

"Size 8." Kurt Cobain-dude took them off the pedestal shelf.

"What size shoe do you wear, princess?" Ben turned to me.

What? What was he doing? This wasn't my style. Not even in high school. I opted for the preppy *Clueless* fashion—short skirts and platform heels to fit in with my friends. I'd never wear boots like that.

I squinted at him. "Eight."

He handed them to me and winked.

"Ben, these aren't my style," I said.

"You sure about that?" His eyes twinkled. "You've been wearing an awful lot of black lately."

I peered down at my cardigan, leggings, and ankle boots. All black. "They *are* kind of badass," I admitted.

The grunge girls at the mall back in my high school days all seemed so free with whatever color they'd wanted to dye their hair and their piercings. I considered getting a little diamond for my nose. I even made an appointment at a store but chickened out.

Well, maybe now it was time to reclaim some of that long-ago desire.

*Decision made.* I sat on the bench and took off my *Prada* boots with the pointed toe and kitten heel, trading them for the clunky, lace-up platform-soled monstrosities.

I stood, and the two men eyed me from head to toe like twins.

"Yeah, she needs those," Kurt Cobain proclaimed.

Ben nodded with that expression in his eyes, the one I was so close to figuring out. "Yes, she does."

Then he asked about some Alexander McQueen, and he and Kurt walked away from me.

I didn't hear the rest of the conversation, but I was blown away at how Ben knew the brands and was comfortable discussing his tastes. He knew fashion—*so many layers on that man.*

Instead of changing back into my boots, I kept the Doc Martens on and sauntered to where he was flipping through a rack of leather jackets, and he was grinning like he was in heaven. A wave of affection came over me, and months of holding myself back from any kind of physical contact caught up.

I came up behind him, wrapped my arms around his torso from the back, and squeezed. He froze with a small gasp, then crossed his arms over mine and held me in place. I pressed my chest to his back and held tight.

We stayed like that for several heartbeats. He calmed me. Holding onto him was a safe place, and there was something else I couldn't quite put my finger on. Admiration? Friendship? Love? All of the above?

I gave one last tight crush with all my strength and backed away.

He turned, smiling. "You like the boots?"

"Yeah." I giggled.

"They suit you."

We didn't discuss the hug and didn't have to. It was innocent, and I'd needed it.

After we'd loaded the bolts of fabric into the back of Jason's pickup, we headed to the warehouse. I kept glancing at my new boots and loved how they made me feel like such a rebel, so cool and badass. Like I was getting everything I imagined.

It was mid-afternoon when I helped Ben unload the four large bolts of fabric for our summer samples due to show in three weeks. The patterns were cut, and the designs were set. We'd agreed to join a video chat for buyers. Only four stores RSVP'd, and the season was making me nervous. This was all new territory for them and us.

The pandemic lockdown threw everything into a trial-and-error way of doing business. We had to show the stores our samples, somehow. I sent swatch boards ahead of time so they could feel and see the fabrics. It wasn't ideal, but everyone was adjusting to a new way of doing business.

Ben... He was like my anchor in the storm.

Standing at the design table, I was finishing up prep work for the meeting when a pair of warm hands slid around my waist, and big, colorful forearms wrapped around me and held me to a hard chest. Ben's breath was hot on my neck as he clutched me and breathed into my hair. I leaned into him and surrendered.

"Can you come over tonight?" I asked.

It was time for me to give in and give us both what we wanted.

"What time?" he whispered.

"Seven?" I said and turned to face him.

"I'll be there at six." He gave me a wolfish grin that made my lady parts clench.

~ * ~

"Tattoos," Ramanda, the fortune teller my mom hired for a monthly night of readings and wine with her friends, shouted.

She had a crystal ball and turned my mom's dining room table into a mish-mash of tarot cards, colorful fabrics, crystals, and gems.

The word shook me from my stupor. I was thinking of Ben, and her exclamation blasted me right out of it. I wasn't there for a reading.

Ramanda recited her predications out loud for the whole group to hear and I wasn't about any of that. These women didn't need to know anything about my life.

This world I was raised in shunned a young lady being in any other state of mind than an ambassador of elegance and light. Cotillion drilled a graceful hostess persona into our heads as a debutante. Graceful, poised, and unflappable. Mom wouldn't tolerate any outward appearance of negative emotions from me. The frustration of behaving like everyone expected me to and what I really wanted started to make cracks in my porcelain doll veneer.

When I was a teenager, I'd secretly listened to emo music and drew dark images of bats, dead trees, and shadowy figures in different states of discomfort. While on the outside, I wore pastel colors and light makeup. I had many acquaintances, not friends. I knew I wasn't into self-harm, after my two attempts at a binge/purge, only outward distain for others who lived the way they wanted.

Brooding and unsocial toward my junior year of high school, my councilor made Mom gasp with the mere mention of therapy.

*"People would talk."* I heard her say that night.

*"You don't pay to go to therapy."* Gus added. *"You go surfing. That's fucking free."*

I was jealous of everyone, like my popular older brother and the girls at the mall, who didn't care what was expected of them.

There were days in my twenties when I'd shut down, longing to be in a dark room, under heavy, red, plaid, flannel covers, with endless rain falling outside. I thought about moving to Portland, Oregon, or Seattle, Washington, wearing black and feeling the somber, cool wetness of the Northwest climate every day to match my mood.

Only when I was done with school and started working with Mom did I start to lighten up. She was so masterful as a mentor to me with designing the clothing lines. She finally gave me some attention and I sucked it up like a sponge. I suppose I was in a phase where I could be influenced by her and her lifestyle. I submitted to living the way she did with philanthropic extra-curricular activities, society events and an appropriate husband.

I never moved to Oregon. My bedding was feather down and powder blue, bright white shutters on the windows, and no endless rain fell in Southern California. I was a charcoal gray mess wrapped up in a robin's egg blue Tiffany's box, and completely miserable.

No one knew this about me. Not Mom or her friends. All of them stared at me now. Nobody ever understood me, until Ben. Whatever the psychic unveiled this time could derail me like she did the last time. No, I wouldn't let her scare me. I was my own person now, the catalyst being a pair of black boots and an ex-con.

"I don't know what that means," I said, my tone more defensive than I meant it to be.

Ramanda continued in her fortune-teller taunt, "A rainbow of a man with his whole story displayed across his body and no secrets."

"Tattoos?" Valerie croaked with disdain.

"You are with a guy with tattoos?" Linda chimed in. "Ick."

"That's what you chose over my nephew?" Carolyn sneered.

I'd texted Mark when I got home that night after ditching him at Nobu, apologizing, although I didn't need to. He texted back that I was an unstable person who should seek out professional help. *Yeah, probably.*

The ladies proceeded to chirp away about people they knew who had tattoos, but Mom's gaze was on me. Judgmental expression switched from confusion to utter disappointment.

She'd commented on my boots when I'd walked in about how ugly they were.

Mom was glaring at me, massaging her scalp with her fingertips, scrubbing, and messing up her perfect blonde bob. It was something she did after she'd smoked too much pot.

*"We all do it."* She'd defended herself when I lived with her.

Not that she had to. *"It's legal, and it helps with the pain."*

I didn't have the desire to explain myself after Ramanda's comment. I wasn't *with* Ben, but I was going to be. That wouldn't be any of their business anyway, but I wasn't ready to admit it to them and bear the scrutiny.

I said to Ramanda, "Why don't you let the other ladies go first? You can have me after."

Before she could reply, I strolled into the kitchen. Made a sandwich I wasn't even hungry for then carried it onto the patio. The cool air washed over me, clearing my head.

Thankfully, no one joined me. They were too busy pounding Prosecco and tugging on their fancy, electric vape pens filled with the most expensive cultivated marijuana oils money could buy.

I could've waited outside all night, but a voice rang out. Ramanda. She stood in the doorway and waved her spangled hand at me, layers of bracelets tinkling.

"Don't worry," she said. "Your mother's asleep, and the rest have gone home. Too drunk to stay awake and hear what their spiritual advisor has to say to you. The coast is clear. Come on in."

Mom had fallen asleep in her lounger chair, and the other ladies had retreated to their golf carts to make the short rides home two and three blocks down as the sun was setting.

A stream of light crossed the fortune teller's face, illuminating her dark eyes as I sat. She lit a candle, making shadows dance on the rest of her sunken ancient face.

I'd been around when Ramanda had come to give Mom readings but kept my distance. Maybe I didn't care to have someone inside my head. Maybe I didn't believe in any of it. Maybe I did too much and was terrified at what evil things she might find in there.

"I've been waiting for a long time to give you a good reading." Her raspy voice gave me cold chills up my arms, and when she took my hands, she rubbed her clawed thumb over my palm, keeping her hazy dark gaze on me. "I must get through those layers."

Did I have layers? I wasn't supposed to. I was expected to be shallow and transparent. Marriage, babies, charity functions, shopping, Botox, and a personal trainer. Period, that was it. Maybe tennis and hidden bottles of Xanax in every designer handbag.

"Good luck," I quipped.

She smirked and peered at my hands. "Ask me a question in your head."

I closed my eyes, and nothing came, just mumbled voices that I couldn't decipher.

*"I'll be there at six."*

Ramanda gasped and dropped my hands, glaring at me.

"He's giving you a heart that could break. That *you* could break." She pushed her finger through the lit flame and glanced at it, then showed it to me with a black streak across it. "Now you." She took my finger and pushed it through the flame.

"Hey," I barked, then felt silly because it didn't hurt. I held the finger to my face, and there was no black streak. I showed it to her, and she nodded. "So? What does that mean?"

"You don't desire to hurt him, but you still could."

I scoffed. "Can you be more specific?"

Chuckling, she shook her head. "No, it's all up to you. The rainbow man has shown you friendship and loyalty. Make sure you give it in return."

*I'm not Rainbow Dash. You are.*

"Of course." I'd fully expected to return all the gifts Ben had selflessly given me.

"Make sure you do, or else he will go away," she said.

"He won't. He wants me."

I was sure there was a real connection beyond our sexual attraction. We were friends; adding sex would be more like love. I was going to find out tonight.

"Yes, he does want you. Please reassure him that he deserves your love."

"Love?" I swallowed, but my throat dried up like the desert.

"Love, friendship, loyalty—balance, and harmony are magic. It's all up to you, princess."

*Princess?*

I gasped at that reference. She'd almost sounded like him when she'd said it—all deep and growly. And she knew it by the way she smirked.

I stared at my unscathed finger. I was going to tell him how much he meant to me.

"One more thing." She took my hand again. Her face tensed, and her clawed thumb dug into my palm. "There's a child who isn't yours—yet."

"That's ridiculous. I'm not fit to be a mother. You, of all people, know the universe put a stop to that." I said to Ramanda. She knew exactly what I was talking about.

"I still see it." She pointed to my palm. "You're going to keep the child."

I rolled my eyes. "Whatever."

I pushed aside that last bit, helped the old woman gather her things, and stacked them in her car. Mom was snoring. Not wishing to disturb her, I turned off the lights and locked the door behind me as I left.

Driving home, I thought about Ben's daughter. That was something I was choosing to ignore. He didn't have to see her. Many men moved on with their lives, not acknowledging their kids and starting over.

I sometimes wished Dad had left when I was younger. He'd made Mom so miserable when he'd belittled her. I'd realized recently that was his defense mechanism. Mom was smarter and stronger, and that had intimidated him. Bringing her down made him feel better. David had done the same to me on more than one occasion, including in front of his friends.

Dad started taking off for weeks at a time after Mom left the business. He'd chase the waves around the world with the windfall of cash from Walmart. I was happiest when he was gone because he'd challenge every design decision when he was in the warehouse. He brought a dark cloud over the place, and everybody sensed it.

After our shouting matches, he'd lock himself in his office and had done God-knew-what in there for hours. He'd never allow Ben to be as involved in the designs as I had. I was glad Dad was gone, but I still needed his signature. If I could take control of the business, have Ben, and avoid societal events, for the rest of my life it could be perfect.

I had to see my rainbow man, touch, and kiss him, and have him inside me again.

# Chapter Thirteen

*Ben*

Two hours ago, I left Lisa at the warehouse, went home, and worked out, which didn't help my anxious mood. I took a long shower. Tried Jason's stupid breathing trick. Nothing worked. My heart wouldn't stop thumping. Every time I heard the words, *"Can you come over tonight?"* waves of heat crashed inside and made my cock rock hard.

Holding her was the most intimate thing I'd experienced with clothes on, and I was sure that once I had her in bed tonight, I wouldn't be able to let her get away from me. Every nerve in my brain and body was on overload like I was frying through my skin.

I took another shower. The hockey game on the TV didn't hold my attention. I swept and mopped the kitchen, organized my sock drawer, went to the weight bench, and pressed two hundred, three hundred, ten, twenty, thirty reps. Then had to take another shower.

It was finally time to head over to her house.

I hadn't ridden my motorcycle in days, and it felt unsettling being exposed without Jason's big pickup truck.

"I've never been in a pickup truck," Lisa had said.

That was weird. I guessed she didn't know anybody who had a pickup. It was a worker's vehicle belonging to someone who got their hands dirty and didn't wear a suit to an office.

Yet, she'd taken me to that thrift store when she wouldn't have shopped there herself. She did it for me and craved a little taste of what another world would be like. My world. Those boots were the hottest thing she'd worn so far. Not her Prada's or her AG jeans, nope. Those Doc Martens were fucking fire.

She opened the door in that skimpy tank top and the same black leggings from earlier, barefoot, as her porchlight illuminated and lit her up like an angel.

The sight of her made me speechless. Every muscle in my body torqued into one goal: to fuck the living shit out of her, finally.

"Whoa, big guy." She raised her hands and backed away giggling when I approached her like a tiger about to pounce. "Ben, be gentle."

I growled, staring at my prey.

Before she could say anything else, I bent and tossed her over my shoulder.

She squeaked. "Ben."

I snarled and swatted her butt.

"Hey," she yelped, pushing up on my back.

I grunted and started up the stairs. *Mission: get her naked.*

"I've been thinking," she said. "We should hide from the world in my house for days, maybe weeks."

"Yes," I rumbled. "No world. Bed."

"Okay, caveman." She laughed on my shoulder.

It was fortunate she didn't see my smile. No, she'd witness a sex-pounding caveman, not the love-sick, giddy goof that I was. There was time for that later.

Flinging her body onto the bed, she lay still while I pulled off my shirt, followed by my shorts and briefs together, then yanked her leggings off with her underwear. She was still giggling, and I tried to keep my intense look which made her laugh harder. It was a challenge not to smile too. This was fun.

I crawled over her and wrapped my left arm around her body, lifting and moving her back with me to the middle of the bed then reached up her back and splayed her hair over her pillow.

She gazed up at me with those big brown eyes. "Ben, you're the best friend I've ever had."

That made me pause a second from tugging the tank top over her head, taking in the weight of her comment.

"I love you," she said.

Her words echoed in my head. *I love you. I love you. I love you.*

I crashed my lips onto hers and pushed my hard cock inside her at the same time.

*She loves me. She loves me. She loves me.* I pistoned my hips into her while my lungs worked overtime to breathe. My heart was beating so fast, and my head spun. This was going to be a short go-around. I was almost there, but she had to go first.

Her eyes were closed, and her mouth gaped. She was making a high-pitched, ear-piercing moan. *Fuck.* I wanted to bottle and cork that sound, and when I'd open it, this same buzzy feeling would make me drunk and crazy with lust, love, and emotional overload. I wanted hundreds, no, thousands of bottles of that sound.

"I'm yours, princess." I wrapped my arms around her, grabbing her ass and lifting her hips to meet mine.

She screamed, "Oh, god, Ben, Ben, Ben."

Her inner muscles tightened and choked me, and I lost my shit. Tears formed in my eyes, and my body exploded in flames.

I fell onto her. We panted and gasped for air. Our chests heaved together, hers pressing against mine, mine against hers. There were spots in my vision like I'd been staring at the sun too long.

*She loves me.*

"Sorry, that was so fast," I whispered.

Her belly jiggled with laughter beneath me, and I propped myself up on my shaky elbows.

She laid her hand on her forehead and kept laughing. "I love you."

"Thank you," I said.

"Why?"

"I needed you to say it. Finally."

"You knew?" Her cute nose crinkled.

"Well, yeah. I was just waiting for you to come to your fucking senses and say it." I pushed the hair back from her face and kissed her softly on the lips. "It was the boots, right?"

She laughed again. "Yeah, it was the boots."

I got up and pulled her with me. She trotted into the bathroom and disappeared around the back of the door. The toilet flushed. When she came out, I went in.

"You see me, Dasher. Better than anyone ever has," she said from the other side of the bathroom door.

"Let's talk." I padded into the bedroom and regarded the pale blue and white room with hints of gold and brass.

Her bed was enormous, like a white cloud with at least a dozen pillows, but unmade and messy, like the rest of the house.

"Aww," she pouted, "no more caveman-Ben?"

"Oh, you like him, huh? He'll be back." I smirked.

"Tell me about every one of your tattoos." She threw the duvet off to make room for me, and I crawled up to meet her. Then she laid the silky blanket over both of us and stretched her arm and leg over my body.

"That could take all night," I said.

"We're hiding, remember? We've got all the time in the world." She snuggled closer.

We spent hours talking and laying in her bed. She'd point to a spot on me like countries on a map: the red number '18' behind bars, the gray Batman symbol, a bright yellow sun with red blood drops, the Huntington pier with an orange sunset, the blue wave with the blacked-out skeleton, the Eaters logo, and two purple dolphins.

"You're a rainbow—Dasher," she joked.

I guess I was. It hadn't occurred to me before Chloe had said how colorful my tats were, but I was a living rainbow even though I'd thought the ink I'd gotten was for a tough, bad guy. Now I was a fucking My Little Pony character.

I watched about ten episodes with Chloe. She tried to explain in her three-year-old-speak about each of the characters. The one thing I did like about the stupid show was the friendships. I'd felt like I'd never had a true best friend. Except maybe when I was twelve.

Cody Baltazar and I would go around the schoolyard searching for kids to shake down for money or snacks. Even though Mom packed me lunch every day, I threw it away. Getting other people's stuff was more fun.

Cody had gotten expelled in eighth grade, and I hadn't talked to him again. Maybe I'd try and find him and see how his life turned out. Dad didn't like him, so the breakup of the friendship was inevitable. Cody had taken the brunt of our escapades and maybe even took the fall for me once or twice.

Lisa and I talked until midnight. By then, we were so hungry we had to get out. We settled on a Taco Bell, one of the few places still open. As we waited in line at the drive-thru, the conversation swung to the show, friendships, then asking if she had a best friend.

"My friends are living a different life than me. They're married and have kids, and I don't have anything in common with them anymore. Plus, I think they feel sorry for me, and I can't stand the pity." She said.

We pulled up to the window. A tired looking girl with a Minnie Mouse mask handed her the late night fuel we craved after a few rounds of naked aerobics.

Lisa handed the woman a fifty-dollar bill and told her to keep the change.

That made me smile. She was a generous person on the sly. It didn't faze her to lose about thirty bucks to the tired woman.

"Put it into your pocket, and don't let them see you," she added to the woman.

Lisa glanced at me. I was grinning at her. "What?" She

snickered.

I shook my head and kept smiling at her in admiration of her generosity. I didn't have to tell her what an honorable thing she'd just done. She was a sweetheart deep down. Just like me.

She nodded. "My dad did that sometimes for people when he saw something in their eyes. Growing up with a single mother who had to work several jobs, he'd gotten sympathetic to workers and paid it forward when he became successful, you know?"

Before she drove away, I grabbed her head and tugged her to my lips. She was a better person than I was. I always dreamed of being the hero, and I'd think about being Superman, but only when he was corrupted by the Kryptonite. The good guy was in there somewhere, but the man of steel was too poisoned and angry to see him. Now I felt the hero coming out in me and it was all because of her.

We returned to her million-dollar house and ate on her over-the-top glass dining room table with the gold, fan-shaped bases at each end and another crystal chandelier over it.

After inhaling the crappy fast food, we settled in her living room with the big sectional sofa and huge flat-screen TV affixed to her wall-like artwork.

"That was a bad idea." She rubbed her belly and scrolled the channels for something to watch. "How about a movie?"

I was exhausted and too full to stay awake. "I can barely keep my eyes open."

Neither of us was young anymore, and after two in the morning, all I imagined doing was sleeping for days next to my Lisa.

"Bed?" She turned to me with sleepy eyes.

I nodded and took her hand.

Sleeping with this princess in her cloud bed in her elegant house was surreal, but it was Lisa. I knew her beyond all her stuff. Beyond her debutante persona and society life. She was as dark inside as I once was, but we'd both poked holes in each other's deep pits to let some light in.

"I'm not a cuddler. I hope that's okay. I need my space," she said when I folded my arms around her.

"Good, 'cause neither am I." I was relieved to hear her confession.

I ran hot as it was and having another body against me made me uncomfortable and too warm. when I kicked off her comforter, she wrapped it around her like a cocoon.

She loved me, and we were going to hide from my complications and her stress, however long it lasted.

I hadn't said it back to her yet. There would be a time she'd need to hear it, and I'd become a patient, thoughtful person in the time I'd known her. Choosing the perfect time to tell her would be the highlight of my existence.

We didn't talk about the future or Chloe or moving in together or where this was going. Lisa said I was her best friend and now her lover. It was already a relationship; no discussion was necessary for that, but we'd have to define it eventually.

My old friends from school and the guys in jail would shit their pants to see me in an ivory tower with a South County debutante.

She rolled onto her side and gazed at me in the middle of my musings. We didn't cuddle or touch. We just stared at each other. She didn't smile or speak, but a soft glow in her earthy eyes was pure magic.

"We'll always be best friends, won't we?" she whispered in an innocent voice.

"You want to be B.F.Fs with me, Lisa?" I teased. "We can get matching bracelets."

She hummed and closed her eyes. "Cute." She groaned, then her facial muscles relaxed.

Her beauty stunned me. All her frustrations were gone as she rested. I'd lost track of time gazing at her until she turned away from me, tugging the blanket over her head.

Had I watched someone sleep like this? No, only Lisa could keep my attention that long. Her perfect skin with two dark beauty marks on her left jawline. The curve of her little upturned nose and light pink, rose-colored lips with one more faint beauty mark on the tip of the left side I hadn't noticed before. She had small imperfections, but like Mom's teapot, they were beautiful to me.

Her relaxed face burned into the subconscious of my brain for all eternity. Who was I? She had me whipped.

# Chapter Fourteen



Screw the outside world. I was basking in the light coming from my rainbow man.

We'd spent three weeks together, and it still wasn't enough for me. He'd moved in, and we hardly left the house. We'd barely left my bed. We'd discovered that the living room couch, the dining room table, the wall on the stairs landing, the stairs, and the island counter were all exceptional places to bond.

We made love so many times I'd lost count. He took his time and learned every part of my body, what gave me chills, tickled, made me cry out, and made me flinch when he touched me. I'd explored his body art, memorizing the images and what they'd meant to him at the time he'd gotten each one. We told each other our stories, fears, victories, mistakes, and regrets. We'd played "Good, Bad, and Ugly" and "Truth or Dare" and now had no secrets between us.

Ben reminded me after a few days we had to get out of bed and finish the samples for the sales presentation next week. We begrudgingly walked into the warehouse to find our work in the same place we left it and dug in.

I marveled at what we had created. He was becoming a better designer than I ever was. His trend forecasting was on point, and we'd already planned the next season.

I was so in love with him I couldn't see straight. Brad hadn't asked any questions when he'd caught us making out in the design room.

"Are you ready to meet my mother?" I asked Ben on the way home from the warehouse one Friday afternoon.

"The illusive Becca Tennent?" he joked.

I may have given him a romanticized version of Mom. She still hit her shoulder while walking through doorways. Nobody's perfect.

"Okay, but first, you need to meet Chloe."

My stomach clenched at the thought of meeting his daughter. I didn't know how to be around children; they made me nervous like they'd spontaneously combust into a mess of puke at any moment.

"Uh—" My voice shook.

"Lisa. She isn't a nuclear bomb," he said.

That was *exactly* what I thought she was.

I blinked slowly. My heart clenched and dropped. This was going to be our biggest issue, and if we were to be together, I had to accept that a little girl was part of his life.

"O-okay," I whimpered.

"What about your parents?" I asked, wishing to meet his mom more than his daughter.

"You'll love my mom, but I'll have to prep you to meet Dad. He can be difficult."

Ben had told me about the issues with his dad's illness and their strained relationship before that.

"I'm gonna text Mom. We can go now if you're open to it." I tapped on my phone.

"Right now?" He gulped.

I tried not to acknowledge his anxiety about meeting my mother. "Sure. What else are we doing?"

Smirking he said, "Oh, you know. Going home, getting naked, eating, sleeping."

Now he was showing the same fear I'd felt meeting his daughter. I was taking a big risk by throwing him into the lioness' den. Mom needed to know he was in my life. That I loved him. Any of her prejudices against his appearance or where he was from should be buried deep or blown into the nether because I wasn't giving him up.

He was nervous, and I was too.

"We can do all that in a couple of hours." I pleaded with my eyes.

"All right, but can we stop at my place first? My mother's old school, and I can't go to someone's house empty-handed."

That piece of information surprised me. I thought that was a society thing, the notion of a hostess gift, but here was my edgy North County dude making like a true gentleman. "I'm impressed, Ben."

"Well, I've had something for a while that I've been meaning to give to the right person, and from what you've told me about Becca, I think she'd appreciate it."

Now I was curious. Ben had great taste in clothes and things, but giving a gift to Mom was quite difficult when she had a distinct taste. Expensive and always on the cutting edge of trends for the high society lifestyle. Only the right gift would do.

He ran into his three-story mid-century apartment building called The Trade Winds and came out with a cardboard Amazon box.

"Should I get wrapping paper?" he asked as he sat into the driver's seat of my Audi like it was his car.

"I don't think that's necessary." I stared at it as he handed it to me.

"You're dying to see what it is, aren't you?" He peered at me after putting on his seatbelt.

I bit my bottom lip. I *was* nervous about what Mom would say to him about his appearance. The gift needed to be just right, or I'd never hear the end of it.

"Okay, go on," he said.

I opened the flap of the box, and a wave of relief came over me.

"It's a porcelain teapot." I picked the delicate piece up from the bottom,

He pointed to the gold veins running over the body of the pot. "It was broken into pieces, and my mom learned the art of Kintsugi to put it back together." He lifted his hand and brushed his fingers along my cheek. "The imperfections are what makes it beautiful, see."

It was the most stunning thing I'd ever laid my eyes on because it was how he saw me. My flaws were beautiful to Ben, and I felt the same way about him.

He was showing me that he loved all of me, just the way I am. I doubted Mom would get the comparison, but it was clear to me, and it was perfect.

~ * ~

Laguna Creek was the highest echelon of retirement communities in the county. The wealthy older residents played golf, had parties, abused prescription drugs, and drank like pirates on shore leave.

"This is nice," Ben commented as we went through the gates. "This is a retirement community? It looks like a regular neighborhood."

"Yeah, for rich old geezers," I snarked, and he laughed. "Twenty-four-hour doctors, nurses, and maid service with golf carts and catered brunches, but there is a bit of a drug problem."

His gaze shot to mine. "Drugs?"

"Yup, Xanax, opiates, cocaine, marijuana…you know, rich people drugs." I nodded. "My mom's friends are total addicts."

"Huh, I never would have thought," he mused.

"Getting older sucks for everybody," I said.

"Maybe I should have brought your mom some heroin,"

"At this point, I don't think she cares what helps with her pain. She just tries to numb it, you know."

He thought for a second then said, "That's awful."

I agreed and pointed to her house.

He drove into the driveway. "Should I cover my arms?"

His insecurity worried me. I hadn't heard him like that. "No, babe. She knows you're my Rainbow Dasher. Be you, just be you, and I love you very much. No matter what Mom has to say."

Mom needed to be fair to Ben. He wasn't David or Mark Carpenter or any of the other so-called well-bred men who were acceptable in her world. Still, Ben was from a nice family and had brought a hostess gift that was classy and thoughtful. That was who he was.

Also, my mother had no leg to stand on when it came to the man I chose. She'd married a surfboard shaper from Fullerton whose family ran a hardware store. A rare moment of emotion from her was unexpected when I told her about Ben and his past.

*"Gus went to college," she told me in defense of my father. "Only boys from good families went to college back then. Even though Gus wasn't from money, college ensured he'd earn his keep after graduation. He was going to be a great businessman. His friends were from the families of the early days of the Orange County prosperity, like mine. He'd been accepted by them and was just as smart, sometimes smarter. So, don't give me your jailbird, motorcycle riding-tattooed-heathen and compare him to your father."*

She was wrong about Ben. He was smart and talented and had the biggest heart of anyone I knew. He'd been in a dark place but was finding his way out.

Unfortunately, his past made him unacceptable to my family's society. I was going to make sure Mom knew that none of it was going to faze me in the least.

Ben stopped at the front door, and his face went white.

I squeezed his arm and smiled, then leaned in and gave him a peck on the lips. "She's just a drugged-up old lady with more issues than you and I put together. Don't let her get to you."

He adjusted the box and popped the collar of his flannel jacket up to cover his neck. It didn't hide anything, but I knew what he was trying to do. He didn't have to hide his tattoos. They were a part of him, a part that I embraced and had started to love. I'd even thought about getting one. Rainbow Dash, of course. Maybe Nightmare Moon too.

~ * ~

*Ben*

My fears about getting involved with Lisa rose to meet me the moment the door opened, and I saw her exact face, hair, and body, only twenty-five years older.

Rebecca Tennent was beautiful. Her eyes were light blue, though, almost like ice, and she smiled with no emotion.

"Finally. Ben," she sang and moved back to let us in.

Lisa gave her mother a peck on the cheek, and I wasn't sure if I should shake her mom's hand or also peck her cheek. I found myself gathering her into my arms and giving her a firm hug.

She yelped, and I dropped my arms. *Shit.* Already doing the wrong thing. Of course. *Shit, shit, shit.*

"Sorry. I'm just so happy to meet you," I said, trying to explain to make up for it. Had I hurt her? I knew she'd been recovering from hip surgery. "Did I hurt you?"

"No, no." She caught her breath. "Just surprised, is all." Her southern drawl came out a touch.

"Ben has something for you," Lisa jumped in. She gave me a look like she was reminding me to breathe.

Her mother nodded. "Oh, well, come in. Let's not hover around the door. The neighbors, you know."

I wasn't sure what that was supposed to mean like she didn't want the neighbors to see me at her house, or something. A big scary tattooed guy showing up with her perfect daughter? I tried to shake it off.

Lisa took my free hand, and we went into the living room. Becca sat on her lounger chair, and we chose the couch to her left. I was closest to her.

She produced a pair of tortoiseshell reading glasses from the side pocket of the chair and a remote control that made the fireplace under her mounted television roar to life. I wondered if Lisa had one of those for her fireplace too.

I opened the box and handed Becca the teapot. She took her glasses off and gasped.

"Oh, my word." She examined it all over. "Is this that Japanese art? With the gold? There was a spread in the *New York Times* Style Section on this last year. Well, isn't this stunning?"

Lisa met my gaze, beaming with love in her eyes. We both understood the real meaning of the gift. The gold veins reflected acceptance of Lisa's beautiful imperfections, even though the significance of that went clear over her mother's lovely head. Every time

Lisa would see it in her mother's house she would remember to embrace her own cracks and stunning reconstruction.

"Thank you, Ben. It's a thoughtful gift." She examined it from all angles. "Lisa, how about some tea? Or beer or something harder, Ben?"

"I'm fine," I said. "Thank you, though, Mrs. Tennent."

"Call me Becca. Lisa honey, can you put this on the shelf above the stove? So all my friends can see it when they come in."

Lisa stood and took the teapot. She reached up but couldn't quite get it high enough. I jumped up, took it from her, then placed it on the shelf.

Becca caught my chivalrous act and nodded. "Yes, that's perfect. Carolyn will be jealous."

"My mom did it, and she's teaching my daughter," I told Becca.

"Well, your mother has wonderful taste in porcelain." She'd sent another compliment my way but was it her Southern small talk, or was she truly complimenting me?

Even though I was a bit too warm, I didn't take off the jacket so she wouldn't see my arms. Becca was acting casual about my appearance, but I had no desire to see the shock on her face the second she witnessed me in the flesh.

Lisa poured her mother a cup of tea, and we both returned to the couch.

"Tell me about your daughter." Becca blew on her teacup.

Lisa shifted uncomfortably, and I took her hand to settle her.

"We think she's just like my sister already at three years old. She becomes obsessed with a task and won't stop until she's perfected it. Well, perfect for a three-year-old, anyway." I grinned at Lisa, who wore a phony smile.

That kind of pissed me off. I frowned at her and knitted my eyebrows. She hung her head like she was ashamed of her expression. *Good, she should be.*

I tugged on her hand and faced Becca. "Do you know about my sister?"

"Yes." She chuckled. "I am familiar with her book and her accolades. She's an accomplished woman. Being with Jason, well, that completely raises her to almost a goddess level for me. Jason was like my second son and the most amazing human being. I miss him terribly. You will have to make sure to send my love to him and congratulations to them both."

"I will," I said.

I was waiting for her to ask what was wrong with me coming

from a thoughtful woman like my mother and the sibling of a goddess, but she didn't go down that line of questioning at all.

"Lisa tells me that you are helping her with the line."

"That's right." I thought about how Becca had designed the clothes for many years and wondered if she missed it. Maybe asking for advice would soften her. "We have almost sixteen pieces made, five styles. We were discussing adding a button-down camp shirt. What do you think?"

I glanced at Lisa, and she was genuinely grinning this time.

"Oh, yes. Especially if you have good pants to go with it. You know all the pieces should go back and coordinate with each other. Young men don't like to think too much about what they wear and require certain pieces in their wardrobe. A camp shirt can be worn to dinner, like for a date, or open with a T-shirt. Yes, that is a necessity," Becca said.

Her knowledge and understanding of the clothing was still apparent and inspiring.

"How about the guayabera?" Lisa interjected.

"Well, if you can find a linen blend that is machine washable and not too expensive. Retail should stay around twenty dollars. That's a tricky one with the intricate stitching. It could get out of hand and would have to retail for over forty. Unless you've got like a Bloomingdales or Nordstrom looking at it, I wouldn't," Becca said.

Her expertise and instruction were so clear. It was like being in the ring with Evander Holyfield or another expert boxer, jabbing ideas back and forth with her. Lisa seemed to enjoy it too. Her grin, no matter how she tried to tamp it down, shone brilliantly.

I said to Becca, "There's a new wrinkle-free fabric, a dry weave used in the extreme sports lines. Maybe we could find some at a decent cost?" I glanced at Lisa for an endorsement of my idea. "Jason has one with pockets on the breast and hidden zippers. It's fresh. He said it's made by an Oregon company. Maybe they have extra bolts we could buy and not wait for an overseas shipment?" I finished.

"I like the way you're thinking, Ben." Becca continued to give me tips on the best way to make a hidden pocket and what stitches and zippers to use.

After about half an hour of planning and sketching, we had a great-looking shirt, and Becca was beaming. We all were. Nothing like shoptalk with an expert to take away any awkwardness.

Her phone buzzed, and she picked it up.

"Oh, wine tasting in the clubhouse. I almost forgot. Come with me." She pushed up slowly. I jumped to help her.

"I don't know," Lisa whined.

"Sure," I exclaimed. "That sounds like fun."

Becca went down the hall, and I turned to Lisa.

"What is happening here?" she whispered.

"You didn't think she'd like me, and now you're annoyed because you don't have a reason to rebel against her," I teased.

"Shut up." She smirked. "You've successfully locked in with Mom but haven't met *the ton* yet."

"The what?" I asked.

"Oh, just wait, Sir Dasher. They are going to eat you alive." She gave me a wicked grin.

"Mmm, sounds interesting. Do they bite? Gosh, I hope they bite." I wrapped my arms around her waist. "Come on, princess, let's throw your man to the wolves and let him battle it out for your hand."

"That's what you think is going to happen, but they'll drown you in underhanded reverse compliments then hold you down until you're just a shell of your former self."

"Not going to deter me, princess. You are worth the nasty drugged-up-rich-old-lady abuse."

"I love you, Dasher."

"I know." I put my forehead to hers when Becca came out wrapped in a pastel pink Burberry poncho and gray fedora, resembling a model in a fashion magazine.

"Let's go. Ben, have you driven a golf cart?"

I shook my head.

"Ah, well, it's easy."

"Why does *he* get to drive?" Lisa punched my arm.

Becca threaded her arm through mine and guided me toward the door. Then stopped and glanced over her shoulder at Lisa. "Because I want everyone to think I have a bodyguard."

I smiled and smirked back at Lisa. In my haughtiest voice, I exclaimed, "Come along, darling, we have wine to taste."

Lisa and Becca laughed aloud and in the exact same way.

# Chapter Fifteen

*Lisa*

Ben had me pinned to the wall of my entree hall the second the door closed.

We'd been all over each other on the car ride home from the wine tasting at Mom's clubhouse. His fingers were down the front of my leggings into my panties and massaging my clit, making me flame up. I rubbed his bulge through his jeans the entire drive. We both were way past go.

We were buzzed on wine and sexual dopamine, giggling about the crazy old ladies Mom called friends and the one curmudgeon husband who sat in the back of the bar drinking a beer. Tony Scarpetti, Karen's third husband, was gruff and tough, and Ben bonded with him. They started talking about tattoos and the older man's time in the Navy in the late '60s, he proudly showed Ben the Popeye-style anchor on his shoulder.

The women were polite to Ben and told me he was good-looking despite the tattoos.

"I need you right now," he growled into my ear as we entered my house.

He lifted me and I wrapped my legs around his body, squeezing like a vice with my back braced against the wall as he sucked on my neck. He reached behind him and flung my shoes off, dropping them to the floor.

Then he set my feet down and dragged my leggings and panties off.

He anchored his big arms under my knees and raised me, bare

from the waist down. The way he was manhandling me was efficient and a relief. I was too clouded by desire and weakened by his passion to be of any help. I couldn't see where his right hand went, but the sound of his zipper lowering made me giddy.

Both of us sighed as he entered me. God, he felt like heaven.

"Fuck. So good, princess."

He braced me by grabbing my ass cheeks and pressing them to his hips as he rutted hard. Then dipped his hips and went deeper. I lost my mind to the hot wave starting from my thighs to my sex.

My inner muscles pulsed. The orgasm built. Over his shoulder, I gazed at our reflection in my large, gilded mirror behind him. At the sight of his tight bare ass pounding into me, I lost it. My eyes shut, and I was drowning in wave after wave of ecstasy.

"There, there, there," I shouted. "Please." I was panting and pleading. He was making me gasp, beg, and scream. The hot waves turned to shooting lightning and fireworks up my thighs and spine. "Fuck, Ben."

When I opened my eyes, he was as still as a statue, staring at me. It was the look I couldn't place before, but now I knew it was all his emotions tied together: love, lust, friendship, admiration, resolve, and a little fear.

He leaned in and kissed me, then lowered my feet to the floor.

His phone rang as I trotted into the bathroom to clean myself up.

"Oh my god, Marisol. Yes, I'm on my way. What hospital?"

I ran out of the small powder room off my entrée hall to find him with his hand to his eyes. He dropped his hand when he heard me. His expression was pure terror.

He hung up and stared at me with so much fear and confusion that chills ran up my spine.

"Marisol is in the hospital with Covid. I've got to go pick up Chloe."

I nodded, but his words were coming at me so fast. I tried to make sense of the last few minutes. One minute, I'm having the best sex of my life, and the next, he was telling me his child with another woman needed him to fetch her. One minute, he was all mine, smiling and hungry for me, and the next, he was different.

It was emotional whiplash, and I was so dazed by it, I couldn't think straight. "Um…okay. Yeah. How long will you be ?"

He dug his keys out of his pocket and pulled his jacket on. "What? Shit, I don't know. How long does someone have Covid? Without being vaccinated, that is. She's in the hospital."

"Not vaccinated? Why do you have to go to the hospital? What about her family?"

He stopped adjusting the collar and glared at me. His eyes were pitch black. "I *am* her family," he barked.

I jumped. "I'm sorry. I…right. Of course, you are."

He took in a breath. "Come with me." His face turned desperate. "We can bring Chloe here, and…and she can stay with us."

I shook my head and stopped breathing. I opened my mouth, but nothing came out. I was going to suffocate.

*No, no children in my house. They break things.*

"What? What are you thinking?" He waited for me to say something.

"I…I can't have her here. She—"

"This is my daughter. She needs me, Lisa. You didn't think this was going to come up at some point?"

He was so angry. His voice was as sharp as a razor. How could I get him to go back to how he was before, back to kissing and teasing me? His chest rose and fell.

"Ben…" I pleaded.

He shook his head. Desperation was all over his face. His hands came up and cupped my cheeks. "You love me. You love *all* of me, damn it. The good, the bad, and the ugly *remember*? Every part of my life."

I couldn't hear his words and only imagined being responsible for a helpless human being when I could barely take care of myself. What if something happened to her in my presence? What if she swallowed something and started choking or ate laundry bleach? I couldn't be a caretaker.

"I c-can't." I whimpered.

He let me go and stepped away in shock and disappointment. "I don't have time for your shit. I've got to go. Just know that I'm *not* coming back. Figure it out, Lisa. This is what my life is, not the fantasy we've had the past three weeks."

Memories flashed through my mind: his face between my legs before I'd even woken up properly. Pushing me up against the wall of my shower. Finding his secret ticklish spots and making a pact not to torture him. Discovering the best taco places up and down the coast to the Mexico border on the back of his motorcycle.

I'd started smelling like him from holding onto him on his motorcycle, wearing leather, and getting the fresh air embedded in my skin. He was leaving and not coming back because I couldn't be around a child? I must tell him I was wrong before he walked out the door, but I was frozen.

Damn, why couldn't I speak up?

I had to compromise, but the words just wouldn't come. He glared at me one last time as if giving me one more chance to come with him or explain myself, but when I stayed silent, that was it. He blasted curses at me, then punched the wall, making a hole before throwing my big oak door open and slamming it behind him.

I still felt his hands on my face as I slid down the wall. My legs had given out, my whole world had just shattered into a million pieces, and there wasn't enough gold glue in the universe to put it back together.

*I'm not coming back.*

I didn't know how long I'd sat there with the words echoing in my head. My phone dinged from my purse I'd dropped by the front door with reckless abandon. I crawled over to it. It was a voicemail notification from a number I didn't recognize.

"Hi, honey, I had to let you know that anything you may hear about me isn't true. I trusted the wrong people, and it was best for everyone for me to go away." My father sighed. "Please tell your mother I'm collecting seashells. And be careful."

End message.

*What in the hell is happening?*

# Chapter Sixteen

*Ben*

This was coming, I knew it was, but I'd ignored my gut about when and how.

I didn't even put my helmet on, and the rain started. Fuck, I wish I wasn't on my motorcycle. Chloe had to have at least one parent who wasn't in the hospital. My baby needed me.

*Get home safe.*

*Get Dad's car.*

*Put in the car seat.*

*Get to the hospital.*

It was a simple but important task list. I had to focus on the wet streets and not on Lisa's reaction to my situation. She was selfish. I knew she'd show that side of her eventually. I'd been there once upon a time when my insecurities and fear consumed me, and I'd pushed everyone away. I knew exactly what she was doing, but would she get out of her dammed head and realize she had to accept my real life?

I rode up to the carport where Dad's ivory, four-door sedan sat, dry and glowing like a reliable and steady beacon of hope.

I remembered him picking me up from jail the second time. I was released on bail, and Shelly had negotiated for me to go to a rehab facility instead of prison. The brand-new Toyota Camry hadn't even had its license plates yet.

He had called me earlier that day. He'd wanted to show it to me and asked if he could come by the gym I was working at. I had a deal to make and couldn't let him see what I was doing, selling Rohypnol and GHB—the drugs used by bodybuilders after steroids were made illegal.

We were blindsided by a raid, and I was hauled off to the Huntington PD.

Dad was at the front desk when I came out. He shook hands with the officer behind the counter and two other uniforms, thanking them and calling them by their names on their badges respectfully.

Seeing that shiny white car and Dad that day made me feel lucky and safe. He didn't speak to me all the way home, and I'd gone straight to my room. Ever since that day, I had a love for that lame middle-class car and Dad too. He always came for me, no matter how much trouble I'd gotten into.

My baby will be safe in that car and with me in my grandmother's apartment, safe from the rain and the virus and from anything else that may harm her. I would always come for her, no matter what.

I already had an extra room for her with a toddler bed and *My Little Pony* fleece blanket for her to feel safe.

She must be so scared.

I threw on a black gator mask Lisa had gotten for me with the skull face and pulled it over my nose as I jumped out of the car, ran into the emergency room, and up to the glass window.

"Marisol Taveras, I'm her daughter's father. Please." I panted, not even knowing if the tired woman behind the glass could hear me or knew what the fuck I was talking about.

She picked up the phone too slowly. She was going to set me off if she kept up her sloth-like motions.

"Chloe, her name is Chloe Taveras-Stringer. My daughter. Her mother, Marisol, has Covid. I came to take my little girl home."

I took my driver's license out of my wallet and slid it under the partition.

The woman turned away and spoke into the phone. I glanced back to the packed room, and at least half of the people were coughing uncontrollably. I had to get Chloe out of here as soon as possible.

"Please," I begged the woman who had gotten off the phone and was tapping her computer keys. "Where is my daughter? Tell me." I slammed my fist on the partition.

"Step back, sir." She glared at me, and the scowl on her face made me pause. She was full of rage and wasn't going to let anyone mess with her like a mama wolf with her teeth bared to a predator.

"Please," I begged.

"I am trying to find her, sir, but you cannot harass me into making it happen any faster."

I was powerless. I had the urge to hit something or someone.

My efforts to be the hero to the women in my life had sunk into a deep pit of darkness. All I could do was wait. At least I could save Chloe. She still loved me.

Pacing like a caged animal, I tried to think if I could talk to someone besides the woman at the desk, anyone who might have answers. I just had to do something.

*"You want to fix me."*

*"No, I don't. I like you like this."*

I knew Lisa was going to rip my heart out. It was my fault for blindly handing it to her. I didn't just hand it to her, I shoved it down her throat. I'd bulldozed her flimsy house of cards, and now it all came down in a spectacular explosion with the Queen of Hearts lying atop the carnage.

It happened so fast. Why couldn't she see how much Chloe meant to me? Lisa couldn't make me choose. She just couldn't. Chloe was my daughter. There was no choice.

I bowed my head and shut my eyes. I prayed and hoped against hope that somehow Lisa would understand.

Before I knew it, an hour had passed. Still no word. I stood at the partition. No one was sitting in the chair. There was no one to shout at.

"Fuck," I shouted to no one. Only a few wretched faces glanced up at my outburst.

I called Marisol.

It went to voicemail. "Fuck, fuck."

Then my phone rang.

"Mr. Stringer?" a woman asked.

"Yes, yes, it's me," I said.

"Are you here to collect Chloe?"

"Yes, I'm here. I've been in the emergency room for an hour." My voice shook.

"I apologize," she said. "Please go to Building C, the fourth floor. They will administer a flash test, then you can collect your daughter. Bring identification, and we will provide a mask."

I finally let out a long breath. "I'm on my way."

~ * ~

After Chloe was fed, lying on my couch with her pony dolls lined up on the coffee table, and we'd watched our third Disney movie, I thought she'd fall asleep. Her eyes were wide open, and she sucked on her thumb. Thank God she had tested negative for the virus. She was safe, sound, and with me.

Poor Marisol.

I texted back and forth with Shelly, Mom, and Marisol's mom, then went down a social media rabbit hole, trying to find people from high school I'd lost touch with.

Anything to take my mind off Lisa and her stupid issues.

Finally, around midnight, Chloe's eyes closed, and I carried her into her room. She didn't wake up, and I left her door open if she made any noises or had a bad dream.

The nurse had been morose when I reached the nursery, sitting half asleep in a hazmat suit in the corner of the room. Chloe was the only kid and was at a small desk coloring. She ran into my arms as soon as I flung the door open.

"She's seen her mother," the small woman in the big yellow space suit told me. "But that will be the last time."

For a split second, I was confused, but then sharp pain shot to my chest. "Can I?"

The yellow helmet shook her head. There was a sternness in her remorseful expression, and it wasn't hard to see that she meant my daughter would never see her mother again.

I put Chloe down and instructed her to gather her things.

"Your wife cannot have any visitors," she whispered to me, assuming Marisol and I were married .

"Can I call her, like FaceTime?" I asked in a hushed tone.

"Not at this stage."

My eyes started to well up.

"Daddy, can we watch *Moana* when we get home?" Chloe stood with her pink glitter backpack and fluffy purple hoodie.

I was nodding but not breathing. "Who can I talk to?" I pleaded to the woman.

I required answers from somebody. I had to speak with Marisol and a doctor. Then glancing at my baby's sweet face, I knew keeping my composure was necessary, so I didn't scare her because I was about to explode in raw fury.

I started to shake from restraint.

"Sir, right now, Chloe needs you." The woman said it with familiarity like she knew me and what I was feeling, and I deflated.

*Get her out of here, get her home, get her safe. Be her hero.*

All I wanted to do was cry to my best friend, but I wasn't with Lisa. I'd left her. She'd rejected me and my life.

She was all I could think about. It was my fault for giving her my fragile and destitute heart.

Over and over, I told myself that we were just taking a break, that I was giving her space to figure out that she still loved me enough to accept all of me.

I had to take care of my responsibilities. Plus, I couldn't always be the one who kept her afloat. She was perfectly capable of standing on her own.

My life was about to change quickly, but I had a strong support system with my family. They'd be there for me. Shelly and Jason had called earlier and promised to be there for us, and I was grateful for them. They'd raised their kids, and all of them turned out to be wonderful people.

At twenty-six minutes passed two AM. I got a call from Marisol's dad, Hector.

I stared at the phone for a good ten seconds, mustering the courage. Right now, a ringing phone divided my life into two parts: before and after. I knew the before. I've been living it. I knew what it was for me, Chloe, and Marisol. The after? I didn't know what that was. I was terrified.

I shut my eyes. The phone kept ringing.

I picked it up.

"Hector." I swallowed dry air into my arid throat.

Her father's voice came on with a soft whimper, and I knew. I didn't even have to hear him say she was gone to know it. The man's sobs were mixed with hacking coughs. God, did he have it too? He was too proud to admit it if he did.

He'd babbled about what the hospital told him and cursed himself for not being with her.

"She told me to make sure Chloe stayed with you," he said.

I tried to hold back the fearful tears. "Yes, Chole is my world, Hector. My family is here for us, and I promise to make sure she sees you as much as possible." I didn't realize my face was wet, and I was having trouble breathing. My chest hurt, and my eyes blurred.

"I have to apologize to you." Hector's voice was soft and distant. He wasn't the sort of man who apologized to anyone for anything. "I know you didn't hit Mari. I know she was a handful, and you did your best with her."

"That is something I've wanted to hear from you for a long time, Hector."

We were silent for a few deep breaths over the phone.

"Hug my little pony for me and get some rest." His wary voice shook.

"Of course. Please hug Anna for me. I am sorry. I am so sorry." I pressed my hand to my forehead, thinking it might hold my mind in its place from spinning out of control.

He hung up, and I sat on the edge of my bed and cried uncontrollably.

My little girl didn't have a mother anymore. I couldn't imagine losing Mom before getting to know her. I started to find comfort in her embroidered handkerchiefs and homemade ice packs. The way she'd calm me with a head pat and a hug.

I wasn't going to miss being with Marisol, but I was going to miss Chloe's mother.

I picked up my phone and thought of the one person I yearned to talk to and couldn't. Then took a deep breath and called Shelly instead.

# Chapter Seventeen



*Lisa*

Twenty-five hours and six minutes; that was how long ago my men sunk my ship for good.

I hadn't changed positions for hours, lying in bed on my side with the iPad propped up on the fifth season of *Friendship is Magic.* No food, water, or sleep.

I'd sent a text to the number from Dad's voicemail. ***"Where are you? I need to talk about Tennent."***

I got an *unauthorized number* message for my efforts.

I'd also gotten a text from Mark Carpenter.

***Mark: "I think we had a misunderstanding. Can we talk?"***

I ignored it. Another came a few hours later.

***Mark: "I think I was nervous and just kept babbling about myself. I promise to be a better date."***

That ship had sailed. Mine was at the bottom of the ocean, so there would be no second chance for Mark Carpenter or any man.

After the last episode of the series ended, I finally picked up my phone and opened a text box.

***Me: I miss you.***

I hit send before I could have a change of heart.

Immediately, a message came back:

***Ben: Take me as I am.***

I squeezed my eyes shut. Why was I like this? What was I afraid of? A three-year-old? Being a bad influence? I would've taken any kind of influence from Mom and Dad when I was younger, good, or bad. They'd just ignored me in their selfish war against each other.

*Me: Will you be at the photo shoot on Thursday?*

This wasn't over with Ben. It couldn't be. I wouldn't let it be.

Dots danced on the screen, then disappeared, then appeared again.

*Ben: Yes, I'm bringing Chloe. You know, to see my sister.*

Yikes, he knew I hadn't talked to him about Shelly's request. Now I'd fucked up again. Would I ever stop?

*Me: I'm sorry about that. I guess I'll see you then.*

No response.

I stared at my screen. I should say something. I love you? I miss you? Already said that. Can't wait to meet Chloe? He'd see through that last bit.

I searched my music and picked out a song, then copied the link and pasted it to the text.

*"Don't Go Changing"* by Billy Joel.

*Ben: Great song. I'll be there at 2 pm with the samples.*

~ * ~

The late afternoon was a bit windy on the beach, but the photographer wasn't concerned.

Jason had requested we do the shoot on the beach in front of his house in San Juan Capistrano, and he was model ready. His tanned face had distinguished lines, and his salt-and-pepper hair and scruffy beard glimmered in the afternoon sun. At fifty-five, Jason Mattis was still stunning.

A crowd had gathered a good distance, watching us standing on the shore. Team Tennent 2.0. included Shelly, Brad, Ben, Kelly, and now Chloe, in the sand with her *My Little Pony* dolls.

"God, he is something," Kelly gushed to me over Jason.

The spectacle of a professional photographer and the immortal surf god had everyone hypnotized except for me. I wanted to sit down with Chloe and talk about *My Little Pony*. A grown woman, obsessed with a cartoon show about magical ponies was embarrassing to discuss with adults.

I turned away from the focus of Jason in the clothes that I'd designed and sewed and watched as Chloe wandered closer to the water. She was shaking sand from her Apple Jack doll's fake hair.

No one else was watching, and before I knew it, I was stalking behind her slowly, prowling like a mama cat.

A wave drew back, revealing the slick, shiny wet sand, and Chloe went to chase the water, perhaps to wash her doll off in the surf. Another wave shot forward and knocked her down, covering her to where I could only see two little legs fly above the surf, then like a hand grabbing her ankles, she was being dragged out. Her doll fell into the water as a scream rang out.

*No!*

She'd be covered by relentless waves in a matter of seconds. These waves were fierce and emotionless. The screams of a tiny girl wouldn't stop its mission to take her into its depths with the full intention of keeping her there. She was no match for its strength.

I charged into the water and scooped her up. She was so small and light. I tightened my grip on her.

Another wave swept in, and I turned my back to it, digging my feet into the sand when it hit. Water rushed up my calves, pushing on my back, making me surge forward. I stood firm, holding Chloe to my chest as the riptide wrapped around my legs and tried to sweep me out to sea.

"Apple," Chloe squealed, both of us soaking wet and starting to shiver.

The doll rushed by us as the wave retreated. I reached down and plucked it before it was lost forever. When I was her age, if I'd lost Rainbow Dash, there would be no consoling me.

I handed it to her, covered in sand and dripping wet, and she clutched it to her chest. Her purple lips quivered, but her gaze pierced me. She was seeing something in my expression that wasn't there. She saw a friend, hero, and protector. I was none of those things. But maybe I could try, for Ben. I wanted to try for him.

She kept staring at me as I fought the riptide to wade out of the water.

Ben and Jason were running to me, and I threw my hand up to halt them.

"Don't you dare get my clothes wet, Jason," I shouted but kept my focus on the shivering girl in my arms.

I didn't acknowledge anyone else. We were having a moment, Chloe and me. Ben followed us, and Shelly ran from the house with a blanket. Chloe and I kept our gazes glued to each other in a secret bond. Something clicked inside me holding the shivering little girl with her whole life ahead of her. I wanted to show her empathy and understanding. Something that was not given to me as a child.

Did she know what I was thinking? That I would never ignore her or brush away her wishes or opinions? That if she wanted to dye her hair or get her nose pierced, I'd support her. If she had no desire to get married or have kids, it would be fine with me too. I could be the benevolent and compassionate person in her life that would never judge her or tell her she couldn't live the way she wanted. I could be the person to her that I'd needed all those times when I felt alone and misunderstood. *Friendship is Magic.*

Shelly threw the blanket around us both, and I carried Chloe to the house. When we got inside, I still didn't let her go.

"How's Apple Jack?" I rasped.

"I call her Jackie," Chloe whispered.

"Just like I call Rainbow—"

"The Dasher," she finished for me.

She finally pulled her gaze away from me and glanced at Ben, who was breathing heavily. His eyes shone as he watched us.

Chloe leaned into my ear. In her soft voice, she said, "Daddy Dasher."

I clutched her head against my shoulder. I couldn't stop the tears. "Friendship is magic," I whispered back.

Ben wrapped his arms around us until our breathing synced and calmed.

This wasn't the family that I'd envisioned all those disappointing years filled with negative pregnancy tests. This was the one I was gifted with, and I considered myself the luckiest bitch in the world.

Chloe had fallen asleep in Shelly's guest room, and Ben sat next to me on their patio as the sun set in an orange glow over the water.

"I don't want to mess up. I don't know how to do this," I confessed.

"You think I know what I'm doing?"

"More than me." I sighed.

"I didn't even know how to change a diaper, Lisa." He turned his handsome face to me.

*Yikes. I didn't, either.* A chest-tightening panic took over and I struggled to breathe. "Does she wear a diaper?"

Ben shook his head, grinning. "Not anymore."

I exhaled.

"What now?" I asked.

He gazed out to the beach. We saw that Jason had changed into the flannel jacket and cargo pants. They were on the shore, and the small crowd had grown, watching as the orange and pink sunset made The Zen Shredder appear even more immortal. It was as if Chloe's emergency hadn't happened. As if the huge universe-opening moment we had ceased to exist.

To the crowd of onlookers, it was all about Jason and his glowing magnetism. For me, it was as if my entire world had shifted and changed.

Ben took a deep breath. "Marisol died."

"Oh no, Ben."

I had been horribly selfish. Chloe lost her mother, and all I thought about was my fear of not screwing her up like my parents had me. If I ever gave in to this new vision of being a family with Ben and Chloe, I'd need to be stronger, selfless, and empathetic.

His head fell back, and he stared up at the darkening sky. "Chloe's mine forever, Lisa. You know what that means."

He waited for me to answer. I knew what I was going to say, but the words weren't quite right in my mind yet.

Shelly came out and handed me a cup of tea. She'd given me dry pants and UGG boots, but I was still trembling, and my feet were yet to recover from the frigid water.

She faced us with her cup and glanced at me then at Ben. "Why don't you go check on her? It's been almost an hour. I don't want her to be up all night by sleeping too long now." She instructed Ben like the seasoned parent she was.

"Yeah." He groaned and stood up.

After he went into the house, Shelly's glare stayed on me. "I'm not happy with you," she grumbled.

"I'm sorry." My guilt was palpable. "I should have talked to Ben for you."

"Well, I'm over that now, but other things are happening with you that bug me."

"Like what?" I asked.

"You're going to get to a point in your life where everything you thought you were supposed to be or told to be at this age turns out to be a load of crap."

I let out an uneasy and surprised laugh. Was she lecturing me?

She gave me an ironic grin and sipped her tea. "Breasts and a womb don't make you a woman, Lisa." She gave me a good stern look. "High tolerance for pain and a low tolerance for bullshit does."

"U-huh," I said in a bit of shock at her language and candor.

She placed the teacup on the stucco wall and held her arms out to the sky like Jason used to do when he'd be in his Zen mode before a competition. "It's the 'fuck it' time of life where you are free from the expectations of your parents, friends, husband, and anyone else who put you in a box. Now you go and do whatever you want because you've finally figured out who you are. It comes on about forty—if you're lucky—and you'd better ride it, wring it out for everything it gives. That'll bring you closer to yourself, but you have to let it all go and say, 'fuck it,' or it won't work. I'll tell you, though, it's truly liberating."

"So, I'm allowed to say fuck it?" I pursed my lips.

"Say it." Shelly grinned. "Do it."

I froze. The consequences could be stupendous. "That sounds terrifying."

"Maybe don't say it to everything, but let go of whatever was holding you back. Like I said, fuck it. Your parents can't tell you anymore. Hopefully, you've weeded out toxic friends and things that dragged you down. Now, there's an open road ahead."

"I want to be with Ben," I blurted out.

"I know. But he deserves to have a better you, and you deserve a better him. A better both of you."

"We are better together. Two screwed-up, dark, and twisted characters," I said.

"A perfect match." Shelly held her teacup in a toast.

"Yeah. I hope so. I—"

Brad huffed and limped to the wall behind Shelly.

"Well, art has trampled reason." He threw his hands up in the air in defeat.

Sauntering up behind him, laughing, stumbled a dripping-wet Jason and the photographer. They were hanging on each other like a couple of drunk frat boys. Jason was covered in sand, and his hair was saturated. Paul, the photographer, had a scarf of seaweed draped around his shoulders.

"Oh, no, my samples," I whined.

"Ugh, what a mess." Shelly jumped to her feet and pointed to the path on the side of the house. "Come on. To the garage, both of you."

Still laughing, they followed her with Kelly trailing them. Now it was just Brad, reminding me that there was something else going on beyond Chloe and Ben.

Dad had called me, not him. I had to tell him. Dad must have known I'd be able to process the information he'd given me better. I had to tread lightly.

My mind became an overloaded basket of stuff, unbalanced and about to tip over.

Marisol, Chloe, Ben, Dad…

"Dad left me a message," I blurted out.

Like Shelly said, *fuck it*, life was too short to tiptoe and hold anything back. I wasn't going to feel bad that Dad reached out to me and not Brad. Those days were over, and my brother's fragile ego wasn't my concern anymore.

"What?" His eyes were wide. "What did he say?"

"Here." I held up my phone and played the voicemail.

His face scrunched as he listened. I repeated it before he sat back and let out a whoosh of breath.

"What does that mean? Where is he?" my older brother whined.

"That's all I know," I said.

"Did you ask Mom? I mean, what's the seashell thing?" he asked.

"I don't know. I've been a little busy," I snapped at him.

*Binge watching* My Little Pony *and feeling sorry for myself.*

He paled beneath his winter surfer tan. "W-what do we do?"

He was the older brother; I always thought he had the answers.

"I'm going to ask Mom," I said.

He glanced at the sliding glass door.

Ben held Chloe wrapped in a colorful fleece blanket. She'd just woken up. Her hair stuck out from static. She had her thumb in her mouth and clutched a plush Apple Jack doll, different than the plastic one she had at the beach.

He stepped out and asked, "You heard from your dad?"

"Yeah, but I don't know what he meant. I have to ask my mom," I said, a little breathless at the beautiful sight of my new purpose in life.

"How much more can be piled on us?" Brad moaned. "Like we don't have enough to deal with."

Maybe a few weeks ago, I'd have reacted the same. Not after today. Not after Ben's losses. Not after almost losing Chloe.

Shelly's words resonated with me. *Fuck it.*

Brad had none of the pressure Ben and I did. Marisol was gone, and Ben had Chloe full-time. Where in the hell was Dad? What did he mean we shouldn't believe what we heard about him?

"We just have to deal with one thing at a time." I stood and rubbed Chloe's back.

She smiled softly. "Princess Luna," she mumbled and dropped her head onto Ben's shoulder.

"She wants a Princess Luna doll? Hey, you had one of those, Lisa. Remember?" Brad mused.

Ben and I shared a knowing grin. Chloe had meant me.

# Chapter Eighteen

*Lisa*

In my office on a Tuesday, a little sleeping girl was stretched out on the small couch with her dolls surrounding her. I sat at my desk, watching an online presentation by our fashion trade organization about supply chain disruptions.

During a break, I tiptoed past Chloe to get a cup of tea. The front door opened, making a loud whooshing sound, and heavy footsteps came into the building. I was supposed to be alone in the warehouse.

Thinking it was Ben back from Capistrano, I ran to shush him, not to wake his daughter, but my lungs emptied with a gasp to see Mark Carpenter. He didn't smile or greet me; there was just an intense look in his eyes.

"Mark?" I whispered. The hairs on my arms stood up.

"I tried, Lisa." He stalked toward me. "I sent texts apologizing."

The way he moved scared me—urgent stiff, angry, but to retreat could escalate things.

So, I tried to sound aloof instead. "Yeah, sorry, I've been busy."

He didn't blink or hear me at all. "I'm supposed to be the kind of guy you like. I expected you to be agreeable to me. We were meant to be together. That was the plan."

"What are you talking about?"

"Where is he?" Mark growled.

His steps didn't falter. My only thought was Chloe. If Mark was going to try something, he couldn't know she was here.

"Where is who?" I asked.

"Gus. Where is he?"

His question threw me. Mark wasn't there to take what he thought belonged to him in the way of my body, which was a relief. He was after Dad.

Mark shook his head. His whole vibe was dark and angry—desperate. This wasn't the cold businessman with a three-million-dollar Cape Cod-style house and a labradoodle. Neither was he a typical middle-aged man looking for wife number two. This was something else, something ominous. Something involving my father.

"Now I'm impatient. You're not cooperating." Mark's jaw clenched.

"What am I supposed to do?"

Maternal instincts roared to life inside me once again. I had to protect Chloe from whatever he was up to.

He kept advancing, and I steered him into the design room. My rubber mallet was on the large table, and I tried to get as close to it as possible.

"Gus owes my clients. He stole from us. Don't tell me you don't know anything about it."

"I-I don't. My dad took off. I don't know anything," I said still eyeing the mallet.

"The container, Lisa. Your last shipment?"

"It's in Long Beach, waiting for customs."

"Not that one. The last one. Gus took it along with my client's product."

How could Dad take an entire shipping container? He'd need a big rig, a driver, and the paperwork to get it out of customs. He wasn't that savvy.

"What was in the container?" I asked.

"My client's property. He took it. It's worth millions, and he knows it."

It wasn't uncommon for us to use a consolidator to share a container from China with another company's products. What was Dad into here?

*"Don't believe anything you hear about me."*

"I don't believe you." My voice shook and sounded small. Daddy wouldn't do something like this. He'd never leave me holding a scorching fireball.

"I had no desire to work with mob money," Mark said as he moved toward me, and I backed away. "It's peanuts compared to the Chinese."

*Mob money? Chinese?* What was he talking about?

Did Dad know what was in the container?

The consolidators hadn't told us what we shipped with. Was it stolen goods? Drugs? Sex slaves?

I tried to get Mark in front of the security camera as I backed myself around the table with him inching toward me. Brad had the CCTV on his phone app. I was hoping he could see what was happening from wherever he was.

Did Mark have a gun? Was he going to take me? Tie me to a chair and torture me? Were there thugs outside?

*Chloe.*

His eyes were wide, and he was starting to sweat. "He was paid well. Now it's gone, and so is he. So, I'll ask you again. Where is he?"

My mind raced as it tried to piece together everything. If we'd shared a container from China with another company's somehow illegal goods, they'd paid Dad for his signature and his silence. Now both had disappeared.

*This was bad.*

But my focus was on Chloe's safety. I needed to get Mark away. Preferably far from the building. Even better if he was knocked out cold.

I stopped at the far end of the table with my mallet in view and the camera angled on us. "Mark, I don't know anything, and you're scaring me. Do you want me to tell your aunt?"

He didn't reply, not that I expected him to. Calling his aunt was a last-ditch effort. This was now beyond high society impropriety and scandal. This was a desperate man and millions of dollars.

He inched closer and backed me against the wall then took a deep breath in, and out. "This was supposed to be simple. You were going to go home with me that night, then I'd get my information. Easy. You're not smart enough to resist my advances if I promised you the life you expected. You're just like all the others who crave financial stability, money to shop, and a good standing in your social life, but you fucking took off on me."

I let out a nervous snort-laugh. I did ditch him. *Good for me.*

"What is wrong with you?" He scowled.

"You're not my type anymore."

I was pinned to the wall.

"Yes, I am, and you know it." He leaned in and sniffed me.

My stomach turned over, and I wanted to puke. I tried to shove him away, but he was implacable. His eyes had gone pitch black, and if I thought he looked vile and angry before, that was nothing compared to now. I refused to cower. I wouldn't cry out. I couldn't. Chloe could wake up.

Pressed up against me, his expression turned sour, kneading my breasts, hard and dominating. He was hurting me. It wasn't meant to feel good. It was meant to punish.

Different from how Ben pinned me to a wall several times. No, this was aggressive and scary.

"Give in, Lisa," Mark said.

I wasn't sure what to do. I hoped things didn't escalate, that he'd realize how he was scaring me and back off. Should I submit to him and make sure Chloe didn't hear? Or do I fight back? I wasn't taught to fight back against men like him. He was from a good family, had money, and a top-notch education. He'd be a good husband and father.

"Get off me. I can't give you what I don't have," I said, my teeth clenched.

I wasn't the submissive, good wife anymore. I wasn't listening to Mom, Dad, Uncle Steve, friends, or David. I didn't want Mark Carpenter or any guys like him. I was in 'fuck it' mode.

"You want this," he hissed in my ear.

"You're mistaken." I felt as cold as steel and needed to project that to him.

I gave him a second to back away, but he didn't.

There was no way I was physically strong enough to push him away. I was glad he didn't have my hands because as my fists clenched at my side, I'd traced my fingers over the outline of my Singer scissors in my left pants pocket. I could do it, I could jam the blades into his body. It would be brutal and vicious, and I hated blood, but mine was starting to boil.

Over the past few months with Ben, I'd calmed my rage at the world and especially at men. Dad had put me in this situation, and Mark had pushed me past my breaking point.

If I could get the scissors in my hand, then what? Where do I strike? His thigh, side, or stomach? The thought made me wonder if I was capable of such violence against another human instead of just beating a steering wheel or the design table.

I slipped my hand into my pocket and wrapped my fingers around the closed base with the sharp tip pointed down when he was ripped backward. His hot breath was gone from my face.

He flew onto the green cutting table, and rainbow-inked arms wailed blows to his body.

"Ben," I shrieked. My voice was unrecognizable, full of so many different emotions.

Ben was pummeling him. Like a wild, enraged animal, he wasn't letting up.

"Okay, stop. Stop," I shouted. "Don't be that guy, Ben. Let him go now."

Ben punched him again.

"Please. Ben. Listen to me. I'm all right. It's over. It's over."

Finally, he glanced at me. His eyes were filled with rage but also regret.

"It's okay," I whispered.

Ben slowly climbed off Mark. He was battered and bloody, but I didn't have too much remorse. Mark was about to force himself on me.

"I could've killed him." Ben gazed at me with those multi-colored eyes.

I placed my hands on his heaving chest. "But you didn't."

"Are you all right?" he asked.

My eyes closed and I nodded, even though I wasn't fine. My stomach was a twisted bundle of nerves from the past five minutes loosening and ready to spew the bile it held at bay. What if Mark pressed charges? Ben would go back to jail. Hopefully, the security camera got all of it.

"Chloe." Ben's face changed from rage to fear.

"She's in my office. She's fine."

He exhaled, and his shoulders dropped. "I forgot to count to ten."

Mark moaned. Ben and I glanced over at him—a bloody, messy pulp of a human.

"Uh, I think we have a big problem." Ben stroked my cheek delicately with the back of his hand and in such contrast to the rage monster he'd just been.

Up to now, the worst decision I'd ever made was getting my bangs cut before my senior portraits in high school. *What was I thinking?* This was the new winner.

We had Mark's hands and legs bound in zip ties, still lying on the table. I'd given him some pain pills and cleaned his face, but his eye was swollen shut. He kept moaning.

"I could call our consolidator, or Mom, or the police," I said.

"Those are the choices here?" Ben cracked open the door to my office. Chloe watched her iPad with headphones over her ears, so she didn't hear anything.

She was such a self-sufficient child that she'd stay in bed and watch her shows until someone came and got her.

He closed the door before she could see him.

"I'm calling my mom." I tapped on my phone.

She answered after two excruciatingly long rings. "I'm going to be blunt here, Mom. Where's Dad? He said he was collecting seashells. I know you know what that means."

Silence.

"Tell me, Mom. I've got a guy here who might send someone to kill him. He said Dad stole millions of dollars of some Chinese product from our consolidated container," I continued.

"Gus did a deal with the Chinese?" Mom asked.

"Apparently, then he stole their stuff," I added.

"Gus, you idiot." Mom let out an exasperated breath. "He couldn't steal anything. He doesn't have that kind of planning or the resources."

"So, who did then?" I asked.

No answer. Was she thinking about who to blame? Did she realize it had to be Dad? Why wasn't she talking?

"Mom, tell me." I pleaded, then the anger started to build. She was shutting down and treating me like a child.

"Steve Richter." She huffed.

I gasped and shot a devastated glance at Ben. "*Uncle Steve*?"

"Did you think he made all his money from us? His mansion and boat?" She exhaled like the weight of the world had been lifted by telling me the truth. Maybe she finally trusted me as an adult to handle it.

I shut my eyes as all the pieces clicked into place. Son of a bitch. It all made sense now. Uncle Steve had access to all our files. He could've gotten the customs paperwork, even a truck.

"I'll call you back," I snapped.

"Be careful," Mom said. "Steve's not someone to mess with. Trust me."

"I do, Mom."

"I'll deal with Gus," she said.

We hung up, and I marched into the design room and over to Mark. "Steve Richter."

Mark glared at me. "What about him?"

"Then you know him?" The surprise that he admitted the connection so easily sent a burn of rage searing up the back of my neck. "He's your guy. Not my father."

Mark let out a little laugh, then his face scrunched up. He groaned. "No, Steve didn't take the container. Gus did."

I shook my head. "Wrong."

"Hold on here," Ben interjected. He pointed at Mark. "You and this Steve guy are in this together, aren't you? He fucked you over, and now the other guys want their stuff. This Steve guy is going to cut you out of the deal. Steve told you Gus took it, right?"

Mark's face fell into a deep frown as he stared at the tattooed, not-college-educated, ex-convict knowing the ruse.

I faced Ben. "How—?"

"A guy I knew in jail had the same thing happen to him. He kept saying he was innocent."

"What a fucking mess," I said.

A faint sound came from the doorway. We all glanced over. Chloe.

Ben rushed to her and picked her up. I followed him, not wishing to be alone with Mark, even though he was tied up.

Ben ushered her into the hallway before she could see anything, least of all the man zip-tied on the table.

"I didn't scare you, did I? You know, before, when I lost it." He glanced at me and stroked Chloe's head as she sucked her thumb.

"Daddy's not scary," she said to me.

We smiled at that.

I said, "You're right, honey. He's not. He's a great guy and…I love him very much."

"I love you, Luna." She reached out to me, and I took her, wrapping my arms around her little body.

As I hugged her I felt a warm glow around me. I'd never known a child could be so easy and sweet. Although she'd been a little challenging at bath time over the past week and woke up in the middle of the night to watch her iPad against Ben's rule of shutting down at eight o'clock, she'd been heavenly.

He ended the sweet moment, saying, "We let him go."

I set Chloe down and moved as close to Ben as I could. I whispered so only he could hear, "I need to threaten him with the security tapes, so he doesn't come after you."

"I hope that works, or else…" Ben stopped and pressed his lips together.

"It had better work. I almost stabbed him. I still can." I pulled out my scissors and sliced the air with them.

Ben shuddered. "I told you not to do that." He cringed.

I hummed as an idea formed.

Wicked and vengeful, I held the scissors up and marched into the design room, slicing them in the air. "So, here's the deal, fucker."

# Chapter Nineteen

*Lisa*

We were kind of hiding again after our run-in with Mark Carpenter. Staying locked in my house for two days, trying to justify not leaving. Excuses like we didn't want any more uninvited visitors to the warehouse, or it was just too 'peoply' outside.

But that was all they were, excuses.

Mom said she'd deal with Dad, and I didn't press her, but my curiosity was getting jumpy and anxious. My finger hovered over my phone to call her when Ben came into the living room.

"I've got to take Chloe to the park or something. She's been on that damn iPad for days."

"The park?" I almost gagged.

I imagined there was nothing more repulsive than sitting on a bench, watching kids so they didn't fall off the slide, or having to listen to other mom's bitch about sleeping schedules and potty training. Like my former friends did every day of their lives.

"I'm out." I glanced back at my phone.

"No, you're not. Come on. I promise to make it up to you tonight." He wiggled his eyebrows.

I was pleasantly surprised at how we'd been able to keep up a passionate affair with a little person down the hall. With her sound machine and healthy deep sleep, she'd made it easy.

My phone buzzed with a text as we took turns pushing Chloe on the swing, one of the most boring things ever. I jumped for joy at something, anything to do besides this. Not that she wasn't having a great time. In the grand scheme of life, it was much better to be on the swing enjoying that flying feeling than having to push.

With a 'be right back' to Chloe and Ben, I stepped away to answer the text.

It was from Kelly.

*Kelly: Are you going to the warehouse any time today?*

I raised my gaze to the happy children. We weren't leaving anytime soon.

*Me: No, we're at the park with Chloe.*

Kelly's reply was too swift.

*Kelly: I need to get something for Brad. Is anyone there?*

She seemed panicked, even though this was a text with no emotion attached, it made me wonder.

*Me: No. I thought you and Brad were in Palm Springs.*

I tingled in anticipation, eager to know what she needed to fetch for Brad. Man, I was bored enough to find Kelly interesting.

*"Kelly: I'm meeting him there. So, no one is at the warehouse?*

What in the hell was she asking me? This whole conversation was weird. Why the persistence over the warehouse? I texted back, snort-laughing at my humor.

*Me: Are you meeting some dude for a torrid affair or something?*

The dots bounced for long.

*Kelly: LOL. I had a package delivered there, and Brad forgot it.*

What in the hell? What Kelly sent shouldn't have taken that long to type.

The stiffness wouldn't leave my shoulders. I didn't believe her for some reason.

*Me: Do you need the security code?*

*Kelly: Nope, I've got it covered.*

I glanced at Ben who watched me with an arched brow. My fingers cramped as I typed.

*Me: Okay, have fun this weekend"*

She was a total kook.

I headed over to continue the tedious task for our slave driver of a little person when another text came through. I dug my phone out of my pocket, hoping it was Kelly explaining her texts.

It was Mom.

*Mom: Call me.*

I'd missed her call somehow. I strolled to a bench on the perimeter of the sand pit playground. "Hey, what's up?"

"How far are you?" Mom asked. "Can you get here in ten

minutes?"

My instinct was to glance at my watch, not sure why. "Are you all right?" No answer. "Mom?"

"Can you come over? Right now."

I frowned. Had she hurt herself? Fallen in the jacuzzi? No, that didn't sound like Mom. "What's going on?"

"Lisa Beatrice, can you come or not?" She meant business when she used my middle name, knowing I hated it.

I straightened my spine, as if she were there, judging my posture. "Okay, we're on our way."

She hung up, and I cut across the sandpit to Ben, who was taking Chloe out of the caged swing. "My mother needs us to come over right now."

Ben jerked back. "Is she okay?"

"She sounded fine but a bit aggravated. She used my middle name."

"Beatrice?" Ben snickered. "Lisa Beatrice?"

"Ha-ha Benjamin Roland."

He smiled wide and flat as if humoring me and my little dig. In our months together, we'd gotten to know almost everything about each other, and while that may have become boring after a while, it didn't make me any less infatuated with him.

~ * ~

"It's me," I called like always as I opened Mom's front door. "I mean *us*."

A shadow came down the hallway from one of the bedrooms, and my eyes blurred. That walk, the silhouette, the faint scent of surf wax and Old Spice. *Dad.*

"Oh, my god." I gasped. "Dad?"

My body froze, and my breathing stopped like I was seeing a ghost.

Behind him was Uncle Steve. Both men looked like they had been condemned to hell. Brooding and serious. Dad was pale and thin. He was always a tall, lanky man, but now he looked unhealthy with sunken cheeks and a dower frown.

"Hi, Lissie-girl," he croaked as if speaking was difficult.

His white T-shirt and cargo shorts were two sizes too big, and he was barefoot, which wasn't out of the ordinary for the old surfer. He didn't like regular shoes and barely wore anything besides flip-flops unless Mom made him. Despite that bit of normalcy, there was something off about him. Something was…wrong.

"You remember Uncle Steve." He stepped aside.

Steve came into focus. He took us in, staring hard for a moment with a scowl at Ben. Then at me in my T-shirt and joggers, hair in a messy bun, no makeup, then back at Ben with his tattoos, and finally Chloe, being held like the precious gift she was. Ben's arms flexed, seeming even more muscular and huge against her small frame.

I summoned my debutante manners. "Dad, may I introduce my boyfriend Ben and his daughter Chloe?"

My chin tipped to Ben, and he reached his hand out to Dad.

"Nice to meet you, Mr. Tennent. It's an honor, sir." He followed my lead as if the whole scene wasn't bizarre, knowing what we knew about Uncle Steve.

But did they know? Did Mark tell them about our run-in and hostage situation with him?

So far, they didn't let on that we knew anything. Just a friendly visit with family, one of whom had screwed over the other and one who stared at me like he was about to cry.

"Where's Mom?" I asked.

We stood awkwardly in the living room, blinking at each other. Dad ignored my question.

"Ben, is it?" He smirked glaring at Ben's colorful arms holding the little girl. "This is my oldest and dearest friend, Steve Richter."

Ben shook the bastard's hand.

We couldn't just stand there. I pulled away from Dad's gaze and strolled into the kitchen. "Can I get anyone a drink? Chloe? Want some cranberry juice?"

I opened the fridge door. Ben set Chloe on a stool at the island across from me.

Trying to hide my shaky hands, I poured the juice and slid it across the counter to her. I smiled at her, making sure I was relaxed as can be, so she'd remain calm. I didn't want her to know anything was wrong.

"Two hands, please," I instructed her, even though I knew some of it was going to get on something.

Dad and Steve inched closer but were stiff and cautious.

Ben stood behind Chloe as if to protect her.

Dad took the stool next to her. "How old are you, Chloe?" His gaze softened.

She held up three fingers.

Dad glanced at me. "She reminds me of you at that age—the little ringlet curls and chubby cheeks."

I sent him a worried smile, and he returned the same. Steve's expression was indecipherable. I didn't know whether to be nervous, angry, or scared, but I was definitely pissed off at him.

"So, where's Mom?" I asked, glancing at Steve.

"Oh, she's around here somewhere." He waved his hand.

"Uh, well, I want her to meet Chloe, so I'm going to see if she's in her room."

I hurried over to Chloe, plucked her from the stool, and tried to appear casual as I picked up speed down the dark hallway before anyone could stop me. I'd left Ben with the men. He could handle himself with whatever danger may be imminent. He'd been around real criminals and had to have held his own in jail. This was just two old men sitting in a retirement community. Still, I had to get Chloe out of there.

An odd sensation drew me to the room I'd slept in. The walk-in closet door was closed. I knew she was in there.

My heart beat up my throat so I set Chloe down, as if not carrying her would help me breathe deeper.

"Mom," I whispered and slid the door into its invisible pocket.

She was on her side, lying on the floor. I couldn't tell if she was asleep or had been knocked out. I fell to my knees.

"Mom." I put my head on her chest. She was breathing.

I pushed her onto her back, and she mumbled something.

"Mom?" I said to her.

Her eyes fluttered open, and she raised her hand that clasped something.

"Is lady sick?" Chloe said from the doorway.

"Uh, no, she's just tired. I guess she fell asleep in the closet. Isn't that silly?"

My goal wasn't to scare Chloe, but I was desperately trying to not sound as terrified as I was finding Mom like this.

I took the bottle from her hand and glimpsed the familiar Percodan label. She'd been taking the painkillers since her hip surgery. I'd suspected Steve or Dad had something to do with her dazed state. She'd either taken too much or was forced to.

"Come on, Mom. We have guests." I implored her sense of Southern hospitality. "We don't want to make a scene now, do we? Come on, pull up those knee socks."

Mom snorted a laugh. "Knee socks," she slurred.

When I got her to her feet, she gazed at me. Her eyes filled with regret. "I know you're stronger than us all, Lisa-Bee. I should have…believed."

Her tender confession would've moved me to tears, but this wasn't the time. I helped her limp body to the bed and sat her down.

She got a look at Chloe, and her face lit up. "Oh, you're Chloe.

What a pretty child."

Chloe stood still, then peered at me. She wasn't sure what to make of the drugged and silly woman.

"You're Luna's mommy." She stated it as a fact.

"Luna?" Mom swayed but tried to sit properly on the edge of the bed.

Two attempts to cross one leg over failed until she, with a grimace, finally got the leg over. She clasped her hands around her knee, still swaying at her waist, and smiled like the proper debutante she was.

"Lisa is Princess Luna, and Daddy is the Dasher. I Jackie, that's Apple Jack. I'm going to live on a farm and ride ponies," Chloe babbled in three-year-old speak.

It was the most I'd heard her say since I'd met her.

"Oh, isn't that fun." Mom tried to open her fluttering eyes.

"Princess Luna was Nightmare Moon before Rainbow Dash showed her friendship and magic," Chloe announced, full of authority.

Mom nodded but her perfectly drawn eyebrows drew together. Her facial expression wavered between astonishment and confusion.

I was dealing with two children now, and I couldn't even imagine what was happening in the living room.

# Chapter Twenty



*Ben*

Gus was staring at me, my neck, arms, then my face. I assumed he couldn't believe his sweet and innocent daughter would want to be with a tatted-up freak like me. "Boyfriend, huh?"

I nodded and shot a glance at Steve, who blinked at me.

"So, what do you do, Ben?" Steve started the interrogation I'd been expecting from Lisa's family, not this asshole.

"I'm helping Lisa design the fall line so she can handle the administrative stuff, and I work with Jason." I added that last part to Gus, trying to plead with him with my eyes to give me some kind of hint as to what was going on.

"Jason Mattis? He's back?" Gus asked.

"Yeah, he's starting a surf school for underprivileged kids. Like a charity. He married my sister." I gazed at Steve.

These guys were ice-cold. I had to assess my situation a few times over the years with the seedy characters I'd been exposed to, and they all had a tell. Nervous movements or facial expressions to give away a weakness, but these two were giving me nothing.

I was used to dealing with petty criminals and dumbasses. Unfortunately, that experience wasn't going to help me with these seasoned guys.

Steve glanced at his watch. "I've got to make a call. Excuse me." He went out the front door to the courtyard. He paced by the kitchen window with his phone to his ear.

This was my chance. I leaned into Gus. "Gus, I—"

He held up his hand to stop me, then strode from the window to the living room. "Okay, look. I don't know you, but if Lisa trusts you, then you need to listen well because I'm only going to tell you once. Got it?"

I nodded and shoved my hands into my pockets.

Lisa told me he could be a dominant prick. That he'd belittled her and ignored her for most of her life. That was the guy before me, but I stayed quiet to hear what he had to say.

"I didn't do dick-squat when it comes to this shitstorm. Steve did some deal with a guy in Biotech. I was supposed to get a cut that was going to be enough to save Tennent from bankruptcy. The guy screwed us out of the money he'd promised, so Steve took the container of the Biotech's stuff. So whatever he says about me is bullshit. You got me?"

"But you signed off on the paperwork," I interrupted.

His eyebrows raised like he was surprised I knew the real situation. "How—"

"I met Mark Carpenter, or I should say, he met me." My voice went low, almost a growl.

Gus grinned like he knew what I meant.

I'm an intimidating-looking guy. I read it on people's faces when they first see me. Hell, sometimes even after they knew me. It could serve me well at times. Also, it was lonely.

One of the things I loved about Lisa was that she wasn't scared of me. She put me in my place immediately.

"I see." Gus smiled bigger.

"What's the plan, Gus?" I asked, hoping the legendary businessman would steer the out-of-control ship we were all on.

He stepped away from me, rubbing his gray-and-blond-stubbled chin. "Steve is going to renegotiate with him."

"Why not just go to the company you shared the container with? Maybe they don't even know what Mark's doing?"

He raised his gaze to me in confusion. "The Biotech company?"

"Whatever. Look, my dad is one of those guys who remembers everyone's names: the mailman, gas station attendants, every check-out person at the grocery store." I peered into Gus's eyes to make sure he was following me.

Using Dad in this scenario was almost as unbelievable to me, but before I even knew what I was saying, the words tumbled out. I remembered the story Lisa told me about Gus giving people money. He wasn't much different from my father that way.

"I realized when I was a kid that it's like a secret power to influence people. You see where I'm going with this?" I asked but couldn't tell if the old surfer got what I was trying to say with my story.

"No clue," he said.

I continued, "If he had a problem at the grocery store, like being charged too much, instead of insisting on talking to the manager, he'd discuss it with the checker. Knowing their name, he had an extra layer of intimacy. 'Now, Celia, we both know that these cans of tuna are on special.'—kind of thing."

"What does this have to do with—?"

"I'm saying, why go to Mark? Can't these Biotech people be a better resource? You know, deal with the actual source instead of the manager. We just need a name."

Gus's mouth opened like he was going to ask another question. Then he stopped and glared at me.

"Who are you again?" he asked.

I laughed.

*I'm Billy-Fucking-Joel-Batman and Bruce Wayne-The Rainbow-Fucking-Dasher.*

"Lisa's boyfriend."

A scowling Steve returned. "Can I talk to you, Gus?"

"Talk to me in front of Ben. He wants to help."

Steve squinted at Gus.

I took a step forward. "Take me with you. Mark's scared shitless of me."

The old fuck reached over and grabbed Gus by the front of his shirt and squeezed, pulling him to his face. "What in the fuck did you tell him?" His teeth were clenched.

I rolled my eyes at his idiotic display. We didn't have time for it. "I know everything. I knew it before we walked through the door." I broke his grip on Gus, who stumbled backward. "I can keep him in line while you do your 'negotiation.'" I held up air quotes like a dweeb.

"Look at him, Steve. Mark will give us the money just at the sight of this guy." Gus motioned to me.

I crossed my arms over my chest, exposing my tats and muscles. Usually, I would've hated my girlfriend's dad to think I appeared to be some thug, but right now, it worked to our advantage. If my 'thugness' would keep the people I cared about safe, it was worth it.

Steve let out an exasperated breath. The rat that he was, he recognized it as a smart move. He cared too much about his self-preservation to argue. "My boat in one hour."

Gus patted my shoulder. I shook him off. I wasn't his little soldier.

I turned face to face with Lisa's father. "Just so you understand, I'm doing this for your daughter, not you. She kept your company running while you hid like a coward. You need to understand that she saved your ass and name. So don't think for one second I'll let you underestimate or ignore her ever again."

"Hold up, slick," Gus said. "We were handling this just fine without you."

"Oh, yeah? Well, this guy Mark's smarter and more vicious than you two know. He almost got to Lisa. If she hadn't ditched him, he would've had you by the balls. So, keep telling yourself that you're 'handling it.'"

"What's Lisa got to do with this?" Gus side-eyed me.

"Go ahead, Gus. Keep underestimating her. It'll only fuel her. I've seen it."

Steve pursed his lips like a four-year-old kid not getting his way. "We don't have time for this," he snapped. "Let's go."

I walked behind the men out the front door and tapped a text to Lisa about what we were doing, glad she'd kept Chloe on the other side of the house.

My phone buzzed with Lisa's response.

*Lisa: I wish I could see Mark's face when he lays his eyes on you again, Dasher.*

I was still going in blind.

*Me: Can you find out what company shared the container? Maybe a contact name?*

The dots bounced as she typed.

*Lisa: Yes. What's the plan?*

I released a breath with a whoosh, a little stunned at what I had to do.

*Me: I'm taking a page from my dad's playbook. For once, I think he may have a personality trait I admire.*

*Lisa: WTF?*

I huffed.

*Me: I'll tell you everything later.*

*Lisa: Be careful, please. Mark's a scary guy.*

My heartbeat fluttered at her concern.

*Me: No, he's not. He's an overprivileged prick. How's Chloe?*

I didn't expect Lisa's reply.

*Lisa: She and Mom are putting on makeup. Lol.*

With my shoulders shaking with laughter, I struggled to type.

*Me: Send photos.*

*Lisa: Love you, Dasher.*

I blinked at her words, my world complete.

*Me: I know.*

~ * ~

Walking through the gangplank gate to the yachts and sailboats in the Balboa Bay Club Marina was surreal. Our feet thumped on the wood like men marching to war.

The wealthy members sized me up and didn't hide any scorn of the big painted guy with the two old men. Clean people in white, sipping champagne on the decks of their moored boats, didn't have a problem pointing and whispering when I passed. *Fuck them.*

Steve stopped at a huge, glossy white boat with polished wood accents and climbed a metal ladder to the deck. Gus followed. I was last up. The boat dipped with our weight. I held onto the railing until the other men ducked into the cabin.

"Stay in here, out of sight, unless things get ugly," Steve said to me.

"Yeah, I know," I said.

The plan was simple enough. I was going to play the big dumb muscle if things got out of hand or until they negotiated when Steve would get his money. Then they would tell Mark where the container was.

Gus would be clear of the whole thing, Mark would pay up, and Steve would fuck the hell off with his money.

Knowing criminals, I suspected Mark Carpenter didn't have the money yet. He would most likely try and cut Steve out of the deal when the Biotech folks paid him for their product. He had to bully the old guys into telling him where the stuff was. It was the same dick move that happened to my cellmate in jail.

It was all going to come down to how desperate Mark was. He might bring a gun and threaten them, or even some thugs to cause a little rumble. Both would be a pussy move against a couple of geriatric pieces of shit.

Having dealt with pieces of shit most of my life, I had to be on my toes and not underestimate how desperate a dude could get when it came to a shitload of money. Steve and Gus had no idea about this guy, but I did.

I consumed two bottles of water and a bag of Doritos while waiting for Mark, who was late. *What a dick.*

Lisa's father and the man she called Uncle Steve sat on the deck under a canopy as the sun reached the middle of the sky. In any other circumstance, it would be kind of cool hanging on a boat on a day like this. Except, I didn't like any of these guys and wanted this over with.

As I waited, I went back and forth on who was the bigger prick: Steve for his underhanded deception, Mark for his lunatic ideas and putting his hands on Lisa, or Lisa's father for working with them both and ignoring my brilliant princess her whole life.

It was hellish hard to choose.

"Here he is," Steve called out, most likely to let me know to stay out of sight.

I stepped down the carpeted stairway leading to the bowels of the boat, maybe to some bedrooms. How in the hell would I know? Like I'd ever been on a yacht?

Mark appeared on the side of the cabin from the ladder we'd climbed up, wearing big sunglasses and a navy blue baseball hat tugged down. There was a red blotch peeking out from the glasses on his right cheek. I grinned with the satisfaction that he hid his face due to my pummeling. *Fucker deserved it for messing with my girl.*

From my spot, I watched him round the front and approach the men sitting on a cushioned bench. He stood with his back to me and sat below the window, facing them. I couldn't hear words, only muffled voices, so I crept closer to the open window above where Mark was sitting and crouched out of sight.

"Well, finally, Gus Tennent, the legend," Mark quipped. "I had to have a Tennent skateboard when I was twelve. I got *The Gus* for Christmas that year. God, I loved that thing."

I peered over the windowsill to catch Gus's reaction. His cheeks turned pink, and he grinned but didn't say anything.

Mark's voice turned stern. "Okay, let's stop fucking around. Where's my stuff?"

"Where's the money?" Steve hit back.

"You got your money. Tell him, Gus," Mark said.

Gus's face dropped.

"What?" Steve barked.

Gus held up his hands. "He's fucking with you. He wants us to doubt each other, Steve. You've known me for forty years."

Steve took a calming breath then faced Mark again.

"I've been doing deals since you were jacking off in the kiddie pool, you little shit. You get your stuff when we get our money, wired to the account in full within the hour, or you don't get jack. Got me?" Steve shouted at the younger man, poking his finger into Mark's chest.

An eerie silence followed as Steve glared at Mark. I couldn't see Mark's reaction from my vantage point.

"Maybe we just go to Visage Tech and deal with them?" Gus's voice sounded confident. He had a name; he'd taken my advice. "I can call Finn Douglas and tell him who he's dealing with."

Gus glared at the man. "That's right, Mark. This county isn't that big, and we all know each other. Finn played baseball with my son Brad through school, and his parents gave him a million dollars when he graduated from medical school. Then another million when he got his Ph.D. to start the company. I play golf with Finn Sr. every year at the Monarch Beach Open."

I started to inch out the cabin door, sneaking around the side in case Mark got physical.

"Th-that's not who I know over there." He sounded shaky. "It's someone else."

"I can call him." Gus took his phone out.

Mark jumped to his feet. He was about to go for Gus's phone when I stepped around the corner.

"Hi, sweetheart," I sang, and Mark stumbled back at the sight of me. His glasses fell, and his cheekbone was a dazzling rainbow of yellow, purple, and green. "Your eye looks much better."

"Wh-what?" He cowered at the sight of me.

"I told these gentlemen that we'd met, and I couldn't wait to have another interlude." Now I was James Bond, Batman, and every other cool-ass hero. I may have even sounded British. What were these rich people doing to me?

Stalking toward him, Mark ambled back like a bourbon-soaked drunk.

"You heard Gus. He can call his buddy Finn to close out this ugly episode. Then you're going to get off this boat, into whatever stupid expensive car you probably can't afford, then move on to your next suckers. You're done fucking with the Tennents. Do we understand each other?"

Mark was shaking, but he still had his witless confidence. He lifted his chin and said, "I looked you up, Ben Stringer. You're an ex-con. You served eighteen months for aggravated assault, then got arrested again in a drug sting ten years ago. Do these fine people know about that?"

I smirked. I used to be so scared of people throwing my past in my face, but now…now it was liberating. Yeah, I went to jail. Yeah, I made mistakes, but it felt damn good to know a guy like Mark couldn't destroy who I was or my life.

Or the people in my life who loved me. "Lisa does, and that's the only person I care about. So, what else have you got? Because I'm getting sick of your face. It makes me itch to punch it again."

He glanced at Gus and Steve, almost pleading with them to help him escape me. His back was pressed against the railing to create as much distance between us as he possibly could. I had the advantage of the confined space. The exit was closest to me unless he jumped overboard. I gave him a smug smile, hoping he'd do it.

"Let me go," the little prick begged.

I stepped aside and waved my hand. He scrambled past me, rushed to the ladder, then did a comical speed walk up the marina dock and out through the gate.

I faced the old men. "Just so you know," I growled. "I didn't enjoy that."

They gave me sarcastic smirks like they knew I was lying.

"Yeah, we know, son. You're a teddy bear, huh?" Gus joked.

*A little pony, actually.*

"How come you didn't tell me you knew the company?" Steve swatted Gus's shoulder.

"I'm still pissed at you, Steve," Gus barked and went for the ladder. "I need some time to think about our friendship."

I followed him. It appeared we were done with Uncle Steve.

"What about the container?" Steve shouted as we reached the dock.

Gus winked at me. "It's out at my old warehouse in Tustin." He clapped his hand on my shoulder. "You got a pickup truck, Ben?"

I shook my head. "But I know someone who does." *Jason.* "And I know he'd want to see you. Maybe he can help launder your karma, Gus, so you don't do stupid shit like this again."

Gus smiled, and so did I.

# Chapter Twenty-One


*Huntington Beach Pier 2022*
*Lisa*

The waves were about two to four feet, perfect for shredding. The Huntington Open was back after the two-year pandemic. We were more than enthusiastic that the organizers had begged us to be a sponsor.

Ben and Brad had dug our old pop-up tents out of Brad's garage, and they were in surprisingly good shape for spending seventeen years in storage. The vibe was different than it was back then, though. More chill, fewer fans, and no bikini girls, but the weather was perfect.

In our tent, we were a true family. My sweet Chloe and Brad's son, Dimitri, were the first little ones running around since Brad and I were fixtures in the 80s.

This was also the resurrection of our brand to the competition circuit with the sponsorship of two surfers from Jason's school.

One of the students; L'Shawn had shown up to Huntington last summer, every day by bus from Long Beach, and watched Jason with his students for over a week until Jason convinced him to join the class. He quickly became a phenom surfer, and with coaching from The Zen Shredder, L'Shawn had mastered the sport to competition level within eight months.

He'd earned his spot on the posters. His mother, Ce-Ce, Grandmother Terry, and sister Keesha were on beach chairs and using binoculars. All hairdressers and made sure L'Shawn looked camera-ready for the press. He was a great-looking kid with the biggest, brightest smile, and I was excited to make him the face of our true surf brand. Dad was uncertain about the marketing, but I couldn't have been surer. Plus, it was time to bury the past of only blond-haired, blue-eyed boys on surfboards.

Surfing was always more than that, and now it was a world sport, an Olympic event. Surfers were of every nationality, color, and gender. Tennent Surf Co. will be the world leader in inclusive surf wear.

Ce-Ce arrived with her mobile beauty arsenal for me because I'd been scheduled to sit for an on-camera interview with ESPN along with Jason and our surfers. She'd curled my hair, and Keesha did my makeup.

I hadn't even considered getting myself camera-ready, but Ce-Ce insisted since she'd done my new magenta dye job. Her work was perfect. She made me look as if I was born to be a redhead. Everyone raved about my new image, even Mom—the highest (and most impossible) of compliments.

L'Shawn's mother had also primped our first female surfer's hair with blue streaks. Petite Lucy was Jason's first student when he started, and after he saw her in the water, he'd offered to pick her up from Anaheim each day to make sure she didn't miss class. She was a powerhouse on the waves, small and wild, carving up the waves like the board was an extension of her body. Ben called her *The Shredding Niñita.*

Our two fresh faces were perfect for a new generation of Tennent Surf and Jason's older, more sophisticated brand. We were ready to tackle the next century.

Lucy's family was set up close to the water and celebrated their girl like a traveling party. Music, food, and embracing the entire competition experience with posters and chants for their soon-to-be-famous Little Shredder. Her parents were nervous and unfamiliar with surfing or the intricacies of the commitment to support a professional athlete. They'd vehemently stood by their decision that she had to finish school. At seventeen, she wouldn't travel outside California until she was eighteen.

Olympic trials for 2024 Paris were starting next year, and Jason was positive both L'Shawn and Lucy would be ready. They had many more competitions before they'd have the chance for Paris. Olympic athletes sponsored by Tennent would be a dream for Dad. He was all in with five gold rings in his eyes, but that was still a long shot.

It wasn't all about competition and gold, though. We were a family, and our tent was full of love and excitement.

"Are you ready?" Ce-Ce twirled her finger around a fuchsia lock, setting it on my shoulder, then stood back to admire her work.

"Do I look ready?" I swallowed hard.

"Yeah. Like you're ready to puke," Brad teased.

"Stop," Shelly snapped. "She looks beautiful."

"Because she is." Ben kissed my cheek, flushing my skin. Would his touch always make me hot? I hoped so.

"I am a little nauseous." I glanced at Brad. "Why am I doing this instead of you?"

"Because it's been all you, Lise. Enjoy it, and don't throw up on Kelly Slater, please."

Oh, god, I'd forgotten that the eleven-time world champion would be doing the interview. As a teenager, I had a huge crush on him. Now, I was blushing and nauseated. I had Kelly Slater's Baywatch posters on my adolescent walls. *How embarrassing.*

"You got this," L'Shawn assured me, and I squeezed his hand.

A young man with headphones and a tablet appeared at the mouth of the tent. "Are you ready, Mrs. Rossi?"

I nodded, and at that moment, I decided to change my name back to Tennent.

Jason ran up to us with an empanada in his mouth and another in his hand: no make-up, no hair gel, just scruffy stunning Jason Mattis.

"Let's dance," he said as he popped the rest of the snack into his mouth. "You have to try one of Lucy's aunt's empanadas. They're the best I've ever had."

How can he be so calm? This was an international broadcast. *The Zen Shredder lives.*

L'Shawn took the empanada from Jason, broke it into two, and handed Lucy the other half with a sweet smile. The two strolled, shoulder to shoulder, eating and glancing at each other.

Shelly had mentioned she'd thought they had a 'thing' going. Watching them getting closer and closer, she may be right. She was a hopeless romantic and wanted everyone to be as in love as she was.

I leaned over to Jason. "What's the deal with those two?"

He smirked at me. "Cute, huh?" Concerned darkened his face. "Are you up for this?"

"I'm still trying to figure out why I need to be in the interview. Why can't you do it?"

"Lisa, this is your moment, a real victory in your life," The Zen Shredder said. "You have been in the shadows for such a long time. It's time to get into the light."

The past year and a half had been the most transformative for me. The new people in my life had so much faith in me. My mission to not disappoint them fueled me, but my desire to pull out my true self was stronger. I'd realized that the useless men in my life, from Dad to Uncle Steve to David and even Brad, had been the catalysts for where I stood at the present.

I may have hated the lead-up, but I understood now that I had to get angry and stand on the edge to get the clarity I had now. The men in my life… I could always call them useless, but I decided to make them useful. To see them not as the enemy but as the gunpowder to fuel my cannonball. I survived their hurt and harm and made it through the wreckage, and after the smoke cleared, I was renewed. Like a Phoenix rising from the ashes.

"None of us would be here without you as our leader," Jason added, holding my shoulders, and letting his beautiful energy course through me.

"A leader? Are you sure about that? I still feel more like a disaster," I whined.

"A sweet-fuchsia-haired disaster." He patted my head. "But a great leader when you're not doubting yourself." He smiled, and I was starting to believe him.

We caught up to the kids, and they stared at me.

They were looking to me to lead them to immortality, and who in the hell was I to be that person? A spoiled, wealthy debutante with no real business training.

"Stop whatever that thought in your head is," Jason said, pointing at my face. "Your eyes are getting cloudy."

L'Shawn flashed that thousand-watt smile at me, and I melted. Lucy took my hand and squeezed.

This wasn't about me. It was about them.

I propelled myself toward the big stage with all those glorious logos of ESPN, the U.S. Open of Surfing, World Surf League, Huntington Beach Surf City, Tennent Surf Company, and some others to the side. The enormous image of Jason on a fifty-foot poster in the parking lot was perfectly visible from the stage. It was inspired positioning from Brad. He must have known it would be in the shot the entire time. It was beautiful to see the Tennent logo so big and bold.

We climbed the stairs to the side of the stage. A girl ran up to us and clipped small microphones onto our shirts.

"Give me tests, please," she shouted over the commotion of the growing crowd below the stage, and my breakfast may have come up a little high in my stomach.

Jason, Lucy, and L'Shawn all shouted into their microphones. The kids giggled to each other. They were excited, and Jason was resolved. Why was I freaking out?

"Mrs. Rossi?"

"Call me Lisa or Ms. Tennent."

"You are all live. Thank you. We will queue you when it's time." She hurried away, leaving us standing on the side of the stage. Jason put his arm around me as the kids peered out at the crowd.

Jason was an excellent calming presence, but I needed Ben, his strength and attention. I pulled my phone out and texted him.

**Me: Where are you?**

No reply.

I peered out to the crowd and spotted Lucy and L'Shawn's families in the front, closest to the stage, smiling and embracing each other like the family they'd become. *My family. The Tennent Family.* I was the leader. Yes, I had brought these people together. It was all me.

In the crowd, Brad and Kelly held my nephew. Shelly bounced Chloe in her arms. They cheered at us. It was all worth it.

But where was Ben? I scanned the crowd and didn't see him towering over everyone, colorful and bright with his red TSC flat-billed hat.

The tablet guy ushered us on.

"Let's welcome Jason Mattis, three-time world champion."

Kevin Bacon shouting, 'Let's dance' blared over the sound system, then the song "Footloose." The crowd went wild as the first beats of music exploded when Jason strutted onto the stage, pausing to blow Shelly a kiss. He pointed and shouted that she was his wife, but he could barely be heard over the cheers.

The men sitting on director chairs on the other side of the stage stood, shook his hand, and motioned for him to sit.

He waved and smiled, pressed his palms together, and bowed like the Zen master he was.

The music lowered then died out. The crowd still cheered.

"Welcome back Zen Shredder." Billy Hallowell, the legendary surf broadcaster, said to Jason.

"It's great to be back, healthy, and in the best place on the planet," Jason responded, making the crowd howl.

"How long has it been?"

Jason relaxed and exhaled. "Too long."

"Well, you're back in a big way, man. Not because you're surfing but coaching. Tell us about your school."

He orated his practiced speech about the charity he'd created and his love for his students. Then introduced L'Shawn and Lucy. My heart swelled. I loved those kids so much and seeing them up there with cheering fans, getting their time in the spotlight, made my eyes water.

Jason raised his arms and spread them wide like a prophet from high. "Everyone, everyone," he said, quieting down the crowd. "I'd like to have the mastermind up here right now. She's the strength we all draw from and our fearless leader, Lisa Tennent."

Jason stood and clapped, and all twenty-thousand people on the beach did the same. Applause for me? Nightmare Moon?

*"Princess,"* Ben's growly voice flew into my head, followed by Chloe's sweet little sleepy voice, *"Princess Luna."*

My smile grew, and I marched to Jason, whose hand was extended, and I caught the gazes of Dad and Mom on the other side of the stage.

I took Jason's hand. He grinned at me, but when I tried to take a seat, he stepped in front of it, preventing me from doing so.

*What the hell?*

Then all their focus shifted to behind me. I spun to find my Dasher strolling onto the stage wearing his designs: a T-shirt, baggy shorts, chain wallet, white socks with VANS, a red hat, and a big smile.

When he reached me, Jason backed away.

Ben's smile was brilliant. "Hi, princess."

Confusion consumed every nerve. Was he here to be interviewed too? He was the style master, after all, and my muse. A million thoughts raced through my head and—

He got down on one knee.

*Oh. My. God.*

My hands flew to my open mouth. Every muscle stiffened in surprise.

He extended his hand, and slowly, like in a dream, I placed my hand in his. I glanced at Jason, then at our people, to Mom's smiling face on the side stage. Was this real? I gazed at Ben: his beautiful smile, eyes, and everything. If love could shine, then he was glowing.

"Oh, my god." I sank to my knees in front of the entire beach and international television, facing the most beautiful man in the world.

He opened a small blue box and plucked a simple diamond ring from it. "So? Will you marry me?"

Words were gone, sucked into a vortex in my brain, but I didn't need them. I knew everything I had to know because Ben made me feel strong, right, and perfectly true. Since no words were possible, I nodded with a cheek-aching smile.

I nodded harder, and the tears came fast and violent when he took me in his arms.

The crowd roared. He pulled me up and twirled me. I wrapped my legs around his torso and kissed him deeply, with my whole heart and soul.

He carried me to the side stage. Mom, with watery eyes, was

clapping. Chloe came running, and Ben scooped her up and into a threesome embrace. *My little family.*

"Princess Luna and Daddy Dasher get married," she sang.

"That's right, baby." I kissed her little forehead.

We made our way down the stairs. Dad followed.

I faced him and waited, but he just stared at me.

I broke the silence first. "My vision of how this is going to work is different from yours."

He lowered his scruffy chin. "I am at your service, boss. What can I do?"

"Make me some surfboards, Gus," I ordered. "We're going to Paris."

He grinned. "I can do that."

I hugged him, and he squeezed me so hard I thought he'd break me. No one could do that. Not anymore. Not ever again.

"I'm so proud of you." He wiped an eye.

"Thanks, Dad. I needed to hear that from you."

He tipped his chin to Ben standing behind me.

When I glanced at him, he took my cheeks in his hands.

"No more Nightmare Moon because of you, Dasher," I said.

"That's right, princess."

# Acknowledgements

I would never have been able to tell the story I wanted to tell without Sevannah Storm checking me at every turn. Her dedication to this project and inspired artwork have kept me going. We have more work to do Sev! "Tennent Surf" lives! I hope you'll stick with me.

# About the Author

I am a storyteller first and foremost. My writing journey began after my 50th birthday and the lock-down provided me the opportunity to get my stories down. Some stories have been haunting my dreams for over forty years. But when the characters began shouting at me at all hours of the day and night I had to write them down, never having written before. My previous lives have been in advertising, fashion and as a small business owner.

I am clinically dyslexic (diagnosed in college) and made it my life's mission to consume novels, poetry, and articles to push past those challenges and tell my stories.

A proud native-Californian, I live in Hermosa Beach, CA, a tiny beach town in South Los Angeles County with my husband of eighteen years, two beautiful kids and two spunky-rescue kitties.

Cindy loves to hear from her readers. You can find and connect with her at the links below.

Website/Blog: http://cindykehstories.com
Facebook: http://facebook.com/cindykehagirasstories
Instagram: http://instagram.com/cmkehstories
TikTok: https://vm.tiktok.com/TTPdSu5kRX/
Twitter: http://twitter.com/cmkehstories

Thank you for taking the time to read *The Dasher*. If you enjoyed the story, please tell your friends, and leave a review. Reviews support authors and ensure they continue to bring readers books to fall in love with.

Want to read The Zen Shredder's romance? Take a look inside *THE Perpetual*.

Shelly is a disciplined, schedule-loving attorney whose has written an internationally beloved romance novel based on an affair she had in the 1990s, her early twenties, with sexy, nomadic, professional surfer, Jason Mattis, whom she only saw once a year for five years in a row.

When Jason shows up to her book signing in 2019 she must come to terms with the fact their chemistry is still as hot as it was thirty years ago. Before they can explore any rekindling, Jason gets a phone call that pulls Shelly into a part of his life previously unknown to her involving an oil heiress, a Central American gangster and his menopausal wife, an antique crucifix, a group of women who are kindred spirits, and the undeniable attraction to Jason that exists after all those years.

*The Perpetual* will make you believe in second chances at love, female friendship bonds, untapped personal strength, and feeling sexy at any age.

# Chapter One

"You made me a terrorist?" A pair of sapphire eyes conjured the memory of a young man in the final huff of an orgasm—head back, eyes closed, mouth open. His eyes had flown open with the deepest indecipherable emotion, luscious pools of blue crashing into my soul, wrecking me, just like now.

*Jason Mattis.*

All the air stuck in my lungs. I might never breathe again. I might suffocate in a sea of killer blue eyes.

"Jake isn't a terrorist," I said, "and he's *not* you."

Any attempt to maintain composure in the presence of this godly man took every ounce of strength.

He straightened his magnificent six-foot frame, still broad and fit, still gorgeous—unlike me. His expression conveyed both pain and hurt. "You and I both know the truth, Michelle. Or should I call you M.R. Taylor?" He glared at me. "Maybe I'll sue you."

I laughed, hoping my voice didn't reflect the shaking throughout my entire body.

Kenny, my PR manager, who arranged this book signing, leaned in. "Sir, if you're not here for an autograph, please stand aside for the others."

"You're done here in ten minutes." Jason glanced at his phone. "I'll be waiting to discuss this." He walked over to the café and sat at a table. It's a crime against all mankind how amazing he looked. He must've sold his soul to the devil.

I looked around. Did the line of women waiting for my signature have any idea the swoony love interest from my book—yes, the one whom I had just told was *not* the inspiration for—was in fact sitting thirty feet away?

I shook out the cramp in my hand from clenching my black Sharpie at his unexpected appearance. *What's he doing here?*

"Whoa." Kenny huffed. "He's not messing around. Who is he?"

"Jason Mattis." I sighed. "The Zen Shredder."

Three-time world surf champion, legend, international cover model...and the elusive man from my past who never truly belonged to me. His girlfriend was a Brazilian supermodel, he'd had liaisons all over the world, and I was just his former "Huntington Hook-Up."

The real man still had a powerful effect on me, and now my years of therapy were in jeopardy.

Fifteen minutes later, Kenny encouraged me to go over the allotted time of the book signing to ensure I'd accommodated all the ladies in line.

I tapped my foot, and my hand sweated around the Sharpie. My mind flip-flopped between dreading the end of my book signing and excitement at talking to Jason. He and I had the most entertaining and sexy banter...a long time ago. Why was he here? Did he live in Vancouver? No, he lived in Brazil. Anxiety struck. Why show up after all this time?

He looked up from his phone, and our eyes met. I averted my gaze to diffuse the sexual chemistry that still flared between us.

After the last fan left, I stood, smoothed my skirt, and adjusted my belt. I popped the cap of the Sharpie on and off like it was the only thing keeping my sanity, as I walked over to him. My current middle-aged state of chubby, thinning hair and veiny hands invoked waves of humiliation since he still looked spectacular.

Insecurities swarmed like killer bees. How did he think I looked now, twenty-five years later? Did he still see the cute blonde I used to be?

Damn it, I *was* cute, confident, and a real pistol back then. I smoked cigarettes in social situations and observed people, gauged their intent like a character in one of my beloved spy novels. But the Marlboro-lite was also employed as a smoke screen to hide behind, masking some deep social anxiety. Jason saw through that the first time I'd met him.

I'd just graduated on the Dean's List from UC Irvine, had a great job as a legal assistant for a law firm representing antiquities collectors, and I was starting law school in the fall. My life was set.

But the beautiful surfer who pierced my soul with his intense stare almost wrecked my plans. His deep blue and bloodshot eyes stared at me for longer than should have been comfortable across the Tennent Surf Company sponsor tent all those years ago.

*I'd looked behind me to see if there was a model or bikini he was really staring at. No one. Okay. I smoothed my hair. Maybe I had some weird flyaway? No. All smooth. Looked down at my shirt. Did I slip a nip? Spill something? No and no. I met his eyes again. He smiled, and a bolt of lightning shot across the tent, hitting me square in the crotch. That bothered me.*

*I raised my palms in the air and mouthed "what?" to him.*

*He side-eyed me, still smiling, then shook his head and mouthed "nothing." That sweet smile reached his eyes, and I couldn't move. He was the most amazing thing I'd ever seen in the flesh. I forgot to breathe.* What's your story, blue eyes? Are you a deep thinker, maybe an avid reader? A philosophizer? A poet?

*A tall man in a large, straw, Japanese gardening hat whispered to my guy, and they went to the far side of the tent and around the back.*

*I padded to the edge and peeked around to see him pull his shirt off. Bless the sheer humanity of him standing in all his rock-hard-stomach, tanned glory. I wanted to play him like a washboard in a jug band. This man was a god. His body put marble Italian deities to shame.*

*He zipped into his wetsuit, covering his miraculous body, picked up his surfboard, and trotted past me. "See ya." He glanced back over his shoulder at me, smiling.*

Yup, Jason Mattis disrupted my well-laid plans that day.

"Since when do you write romance novels?" His words dripped disdain as I sat across from him.

"Since when do you *read* romance novels?" I shot back.

Just like that, we're back to our regular banter. Our sarcastic back and forth was like foreplay and usually ended up with us naked. His voice made my sex clench and pulsate. It hadn't done that in years. Oh, what this man still did to me.

"You read it?" I sat back, pushing my belt tie down again so my belly didn't pouch.

He nodded and stared at me. "That's how I knew it was me. You wrote it word for word, Michelle."

"I did not. Jake's a pilot, not a surfer."

He shook his gorgeous head. "Word for word, *Michelle*."

Gazing at his soft, full, pink lips, I remembered how they'd felt on my wrists, and other places, that first night.

"It was a good story. It should be told." I fiddled with the napkin dispenser, pulling a few out to fold in front of me.

He smirked at my nervous compulsion. "What are you going to do with those now that you've refolded them?"

I slid them across the table and gazed up at him.

He slumped in his chair, looking down at my gift like he was relieved I wasn't angry with him. He placed his hand on the napkins and curled his fingers into a stack. "The book's a success. Congratulations."

"Thanks." I sighed. "I've been working on it for years." I glanced at his left hand resting on the napkins. No ring. "Are you married?" I regretted asking the moment the words left my mouth.

"Not for a long time." He shifted, and his seat creaked.

I nodded, deciding not to press the subject.

"How about you?" he asked.

Surely he knew the answer to that. *Everyone* knew. My *People Magazine* interview had covered my husband's long terminal battle with cancer, my grown kids, nineteen and twenty-one, and even my two cats, Thor and Loki. My sons named them. It's all over the internet, my Google profile, Wikipedia, and my book jacket.

"Not anymore." I shrugged.

"Right, I did read that somewhere. I'm sorry."

"*People Magazine*." I squinted at him. "You're reading *People Magazine* and romance novels, Jason. Who are you?"

He laughed.

I'd missed that laugh, low and husky and with his whole body.

"Oh, Shelly." He fiddled with his phone. "You made me laugh at myself. Like no one else."

"Stop doing stupid shit, and I won't have any ammunition." I blushed and pulled more napkins from the dispenser. "I admit I've been stalking you a bit too."

"Okay, I'm not stalking you." He still smiled, watching me.

"You sure about that?"

His grin tightened to a straight line.

Neither of us was stalking the other. Mine was *research*. I don't know what his was.

"I Googled you and saw you'd sold your private jet company," I told him. "That seemed serendipitous for my story since Jake's a pilot."

"I thought I wasn't Jake."

"Okay, maybe now that you've been so *pertinacious* about it, it may've been in my subconscious to write him *similar* to you."

"*Pertinacious*. What's that word?" His face lit up, and he snagged his phone. "Per-tin-a-cious. Adjective, meaning resolute, persevering, constant, steady." He showed me his phone screen. "Good one, *wordsmith*."

I giggled. I'd forgotten his fascination with words, how they'd turned him on. Another thing I'd missed about him.

*"Give me a word."*

*"Salacious." I straddled Jason's lap fully clothed.*

*He squirmed beneath me and grabbed my hips, pulling me onto him. "Oh yes! Another."*

*I liked this game. His reaction made me want to grind hard on him. "Insatiable."*

*His smile set me on fire. I circled my core over his erection.*

*"Hell, yeah! How many syllables is that?" He threw his head back.*

*I counted on my fingers. "Four."*

*"More."*

*"Avaricious."*

*'What does that mean?"*

*"Greedy."*

*"Oh, pones cachondo."*

*"What's that?" My thoughts spun as he lifted his hips, hitting me in the right spot and making me lightheaded.*

*"It's Spanish for 'you turn me on.'"*

*"You speak Spanish too?" I kissed him hard. "God, that's hot."*

*"Spanish, French, Japanese..."*

*"Oh, say something in French." My body flamed from the friction between my legs, and I moaned.*

*"Broyer mon amour. Grind, my love."*

*"Shit, Jason." I huffed. So close...*

*"Eu precesio de você." He panted as he lifted his hips again and grabbed the back of my head.*

*My heart was pounding for the oncoming orgasm, so I'd barely heard what he'd said.*

*"What language is that?"*

*"Portuguese."*

*"What does it mean?"*

*He shook his head "I can't tell you."*

"Your book was well written. I was impressed and not at all surprised."

"Are you going to sue me?" I pulled the hair off my neck. All hot and bothered from the memory, a hot flash, or just Jason's proximity?

"You tell me, Counselor," he said. "Should I?"

"J, I wasn't that kind of lawyer."

"It's pretty simple. Defamation of character, maybe?" He was goading me, and I wasn't going to lose my argument.

"Defamation? You're the fantasy of millions of women all over the world *and* voted Best Book Boyfriend by Romance Reads, for Christ's sake."

"What a fucking honor. Do I get any prize money?"

*Oh Jason, sharp as always. God, I'd missed him.*

"Jake isn't you," I repeated. "There's a disclaimer."

"A disclaimer?"

"Yes. The characters in this book do not reflect anyone living or dead and any similarities are coincidental."

"Oh, really? Who else throws up when they have a fever because of a rare heart condition? How many people have you known?"

*As I lay on his chest listening to his purr snore. We'd just met that day and he wanted to cuddle. Jason Mattis, the legend, the superstar, was a cuddler. His body was on fire but he didn't let me go. Jason started to shake, his teeth chattering. His skin radiated heat, getting clammy. Perspiration made his skin glow. His head thrashed side-to-side.*

*I sat up. "Jason." I shook him awake. "Jason, do you have the flu?"*

*He rolled his eyes and continued to tremble.*

*"Oh shit, you're burning up." I palmed his forehead and the back of his neck. "Come on, let's get you in the shower." I pulled his arms.*

*He got up on his own. I couldn't support his entire weight.*

*I put his arm over my shoulders and helped his slumping, burning body into the bathroom, where I turned on the faucet. I adjusted for cool, not too cold, got in first, and guided him in.*

*"Burning!" he shouted. "No, no. It's fucking freezing! Fuck, make it stop!"*

*"We have to lower your temperature." I held his naked body under the water.*

*He slinked his arms around my waist and hugged me. "Okay,*

*Shelly. Okay."*

*Resting his head in the crook of my neck, he took deep breaths. Quite a few loud heartbeats passed. "I have to get my heart rate down and holding onto you naked isn't helping."*

*"You sound better."*

*"Yeah, now that you've scorched my skin."*

*"Okay, now you sound like you."*

*"Get out!" he shouted. "Get out of the shower now!"*

*I jumped out just as he'd leaned forward and retched, yellow bile spewing from his mouth. He panted and held onto the side of the tub.*

*"What can I do, Jason? Tell me."*

*He just held his hand up to me and retched again. He bent forward, pressed his arm across his stomach, then spat. "Damn it!"*

*I took a towel from the back of the door and held it, not drying myself.*

*Jason turned off the faucet and got out. I handed him the towel. He looked up at me with fear and humility in his big eyes, then took the towel from me and draped it around my shoulders. He pulled another one from the back of the door, threw it over his head, and stumbled out of the bathroom, falling onto the bed face down.*

*"Do you have ibuprofen?" I asked.*

*"I can't take it. There's aspirin in the drawer." He pointed.*

*I opened the drawer on the nightstand to three empty aspirin bottles. A fourth had two tablets left. "You're going to need some more."*

*He held out his palm, and I handed him the pills. His stunning rear end stared at me. The cream color contrasted with the line across his hips, breaking to a golden tan.*

*"Your skin looks much better," I said.*

*"You're looking at my ass," he mumbled into the bed.*

*"Yes. I want to bite it."*

*He jiggled from laughter. "Where are you?"*

*"I'm still ogling your ass."*

*"Come here."*

*I lay down on my stomach, turning my head to face him.*

*"What happened?" I asked. "You just have a fever."*

*"I have a heart condition, kind of a flutter. Fever could send me into cardiac arrest."*

*What? My stomach clenched.*

*"You did the right thing. Sorry for yelling at you."*

*"You acted like a big baby," I teased him.*

*He didn't laugh.*

*"Jason, you can't compete today."*

*He buried his face again. "I have to." He eased himself up.*

*"You need to see a doctor."*

*"Are you a doctor?" He went into the bathroom, took a swig of mouthwash, swished it around and spit it out in the sink.*

*"What? No, you crazy person."*

*"I only want to see you right now." He took my hand as he crawled back onto the bed and pulled me close to him.*

*"You're impossible." I rested my head on his chest, resuming the exact position from before the episode. I'd just become his biggest fan. Before I could say another word, he was asleep.*

Jason looked at his watch and stood. "I have to go."

"You're not going to sue me?"

"There are so many things I want to do to you, Shelly."

"Yeah? To my *fat ass,*" I mumbled.

"Yeah." He glared at me, serious as a heart attack. "Especially that."

I swallowed hard in shock. "I don't understand."

"Yes, you do." He closed his eyes and hung his head, as if willing me to read his thoughts.

I imagined some dirty ones, for sure.

"Where are you staying?"

His question surprised me. "The Fairmont downtown until tomorrow."

"Have dinner with me."

"I can't. I'm dining with my publisher." I took my phone out and saw the dinner notification. "You want to come?"

"Do I need a tux?"

"No, Nutball." I chuckled. "Although I'd love to see you in a tux, no. We're just having dinner at the hotel."

"That's easy. I'm staying there too."

"Are you here on business?"

"You're my business today."

"You just flew up here to see me?"

"I have planes. I can go anywhere." He turned to leave.

"Jason?" I called after him. "Jake's *not* a terrorist."

"Good. Cause neither am I."

What did that even mean?

# Chapter Two

*Jason*

I still hadn't been sure that M.R. Taylor was *my* Shelly until seeing her smile, her movements, and especially the way she looked confident and anxious at the same time. I'd know her anywhere. I'd known her since the first time I'd laid eyes on her thirty years ago at the Huntington Open. As I walked out of the bookstore the memory came so clearly.

*The last set of the day. I felt like shit. My skin burned, and my head pounded.*

Keep it together, man. *Ma was in a hospital bed with a chemo IV in her arm, and Pop had been drowning in a sea of bills. I had to compete, or I wouldn't get paid. Not to mention, Old Man Tennant would scalp me if I bagged out now. He looked ridiculous with that big straw hat. Thank God he didn't make me wear one too.*

*Everything irritated me, including the chafing collar of my wetsuit. The first one I'd grabbed when I saw that blonde peeking around the tent.*

*How cute she was, trying to look cool with her cigarette, like some old movie character with major attitude. She'd give me some smoky, throaty line like, "Just whistle if you need me. You know how to whistle, don't you? Just put your lips together and blow."*

*Ma loved those movies.*

*The way she looked at me differed from most chicks. Like she already knew I wasn't some dumb surfer.*

*The crowd waited for me to do my thing, the theater my sponsor reminded me to do before I got into the water. He didn't need to remind me. Ever since I'd dislocated my shoulder at sixteen, I chatted with the ocean before jumping in. That became a tradition, a ceremonial understanding with the waves so they wouldn't hurt me. Tennant Surf Co. named me "Zen Shredder." Not because I was some hippie kook. But because that's what they saw when I'd taken a moment to bond with the waves.*

*The cheers started for me to begin my ritual. As soon as I'd raise my arms, palms up to the sky, they'd fall silent.*

*"Oh, great ocean, I fear and respect your beauty. I wish not to take away nor leave anything behind. Only to dance with you for a short time."*

*Some places would be as quiet as the dead when I spoke. My hometown would recite the entire thing with me. Fifty thousand in attendance chanting right with me—there's nothing like it in the whole world. I'd finish by turning to them and shouting, "Let's dance!" like from Footloose.*

*I needed a little more time before the show. The fever worsened, but cheering fans made the best medicine. Breathing in through the nose, out though the mouth, I tried to channel the pounding in my head.*

*I raised my hands, palms up.*

*The crowd fell silent. All fifty thousand recited my prayer. Their wish for my safety in the unpredictable waves supplied the fuel I'd needed to get out there and let everything else go away.*

*"Let's dance!" We all cheered together.*

*For the first time on the tour, I worried about getting sick. If it got out of hand, I'd end up in the hospital, like when I was nine. My sponsors would find out about my heart condition, and I'd be done for.*

The same high level of stress from that day dogged me as I left the bookstore for the parking lot. My phone kept buzzing from unknown numbers. I was disinclined to answer any of them. All I could think about was Shelly and our life three lifetimes ago. Even though I'd jumped on the plane this morning to come see her, I didn't really have a plan. Getting into my rented Escalade, I put the hotel's address into the GPS. Hopefully my Black Card would get me a room, since I didn't book one.

I had to smile, watching her fiddle with those napkins, her energy so frenetic but grounded at the same time. I'd missed her. She hadn't changed since the first night I'd met her.

*"You were great out there today."*

*"It wasn't my best day, though. I'm off for some reason."*

*She nodded with a hum, like she agreed with me.*

*"You noticed I was off?"*

*She turned to me with a bewildered look. "Yeah, I noticed. You seemed distracted."*

*Yup, burrowing into my brain, like she could read the deep recesses of my mind.*

*She released my hand and sidled away from me. "But I don't know you. I might've imagined it."*

*"I was." I closed the distance between us. There's no way I'd tell her about Ma or anything else going on, even though I wanted to. "You were distracting." I took her hand back and kissed her wrist.*

*Her whole body shuddered, then she pulled away and gathered herself lightning fast. "Oh please," she scoffed. "Jason Mattis, the Cheese Grater. You're a professional. Some chick in a sponsor tent couldn't distract you."*

*The Cheese Grater?*

*I laughed so hard I doubled over with my arms around my stomach. "The Zen Shredder," I corrected her.*

*"Whatever." She rolled her eyes, a huge grin on her face.*

*What a tease.*

# Chapter Three

*The Fairmont Hotel, Vancouver, Canada*
*Shelly*

Jason called my room a half-hour before dinner and told me he'd be in the bar.

Doing my makeup, I stared into the mirror at the older woman who'd lived a lifetime since she'd waited for her fantasy man to come see her every year. He'd show up every July for the Huntington Open to stay with me, sleep in my bed, make out with me, but not have sex. He'd had an agreement with his Brazilian model girlfriend, Gabriella or Gabby, to not sleep with any other girl. He'd told me all about her, but I didn't care when he was with me. It was the only reckless thing I'd ever done, and it was only because of him. He made me want to be less of a control freak and take chances.

The entire timeline played in front of me like a movie. Year after year, he'd show up, and I'd always take him in. We'd mess around, get naked, and do almost everything but have actual sex for five years.

Jason's sponsors paid for his meals and clothes. He had a per diem to spend and they'd pay for his lodgings, but he wanted to stay with me every time he was in town. He didn't call ahead, he just showed up with a bag and his surfboard…and I took him in every time.

I loved having him around. He liked my cooking and did the dishes. He put everything back where I insisted it go. He asked about my day and smelled like summer. Falling for him would be the end of me, but I couldn't help it. I was all messed up in my head, in the dark, with him breathing in my ear. If I asked too many questions about his arrangement with Gabriella, he'd think I was too clingy. I wanted to see him, talk with him, kiss him. I was the "other woman," one of many at the time. He never made promises. I never expected him to.

The first year he'd won the Open, I wouldn't have known it from him. He'd left, and I didn't hear from or see him until the next year.

I'd kept our affair hidden from everyone so they wouldn't think me a desperate groupie to the legendary surfer.

My once-a-year lover/roommate left at the break of dawn each day to surf, then he spent all day at the tournament. Little did he know, on the Saturday and Sunday sessions, I snuck down and sat alone with a big hat and binoculars to watch him. I didn't need the binoculars though. I knew which one he was, out there with his elegant balance and command of the torrid ocean waves.

*An orchestra conductor leading the mighty Pacific, creating music and inspiring poetry. The ocean bowed to him, and he embraced it like he did me. He could also leave the water behind, walk away from the waves, and not think of them when he wasn't surfing. Just like me.*

After four years of him plowing into my life and turning everything upside down, something changed in me. I graduated from law school and found a really good job. Several boyfriends between his visits never lasted, no matter how wonderful they had been. The affair with Jason was going nowhere. Just an endless cycle of perpetual spin.

I wasn't supposed to be in love with Jason. My sanity teetered on the edge. I knew if I told him, he wouldn't come to see me anymore. I wasn't ready to end our fun yet.

There were moments when I was sure he'd felt the same way about me. We approached that edge where I'd need to confront him. He'd have to decide, or I'd have to let him go.

After the fourth year, I finally snapped at him. The bar exam was next week, and I needed to study. Not play house with a beautiful twenty-eight-year-old nomad. My real life was starting. I was no longer a frivolous young girl who could invite a man into my life once or twice a year with no promises or future. I needed to think. I needed a plan. It would have to wait until Jason left again so I could clear my head from the mind-searing inferno that dominated my body when I was around him.

The following year, he didn't show up or call. I had no way of contacting him; he'd wanted it that way. In some ways, I was relieved the affair had ended. In others, I mourned the loss of someone who'd become more important to me than anyone ever had.

Staring into the mirror at myself, all made up and determined to finally face Jason, the last time we'd been together played out in my head. I'd been curled up on my couch, pouring over claim briefs of the theft of an ivory Cantonese box worth about $200,000, listening to Billie Holiday, a thunderstorm pounding against the windows, when someone knocked on the door.

Jason. Only Jason. No one else would show up at my house like that.

*"My mom died," he said, soaked from the rain and more beautiful than my heart could take.*

*I threw my arms around his shoulders, wanting to dry him, warm him, and take away his pain. "I am so sorry."*

*"Can I come in?" he asked.*

*"Have I ever refused you?" I stepped aside for him to enter.*

*Even though it was cold and wet, he still wore shorts and flip flops, keeping warm by a soaked flannel jacket, just like the one he'd worn in the last Tennant Surf Co. ad in the surf magazines.*

*He'd given the camera that over-his-shoulder-look he'd given me the first time I'd ever seen him. The memory still made me pulse.*

*"Don't you have a rain jacket?"*

*He came in and went right for the fridge like he lived there. "Yeah, somewhere. I wasn't planning on staying this long."*

*"How long have you been here?"*

*"Since June."*

*My ego whimpered with the knowledge he hadn't called me in six months and had missed our annual rendezvous I counted on, put in my calendar, and looked forward to all year. I wrapped my arms around my body, not knowing what to do with them—or what to do at all.*

*"She had a recurrence of the cancer, and they couldn't get to it this time."*

*I didn't say anything.*

*He sat down on the couch and stared into nothingness. "I missed you."*

*"What exactly do you miss, Jason?" I snapped. He was pulling me in to his control again, and I needed to stay strong.*

*"You're wearing too many clothes." He ignored my question, as usual.*

*He's too beautiful; I couldn't possibly resist him. Okay, I'd give in one final time then say goodbye. I approached the couch, and he reached for me.*

*He fiddled with the buttons of my pajamas, keeping his impassioned, bloodshot gaze locked to mine in his regular seductive way that melted me every time.*

*It took little effort to get me naked. He took off his shirt and touched me all over. I'd gained some weight since he'd seen me last, and my belly jiggled. He leaned forward and kissed right below my navel. Picking me up, cradling me close to his naked chest, he carried me into the bedroom, laid me on the bed, then pulled his shorts off. Rather than climb between my legs, he crawled on top of me, elbows on either side of my head, and stared down at me, silent. His eyes darted and circled as he looked at my face, his hardness pressed against my soft belly.*

*I'd never wanted anything more in my life than for him to be inside me at that moment. I didn't care he didn't belong to me or any of the other girls. He was here with me now, and we both wanted this. I'd waited long enough.*

*I wrapped my legs around his torso to signal I was open and wanted him, all up to him now.*

*His cock twitched at my wetness, and he inched closer, his eyes becoming dark and glassy, never leaving mine. Heartbeats passed as he looked down at me.*

Yes. *No words were spoken.* Beat. *He inhaled.* You have to choose. *His tip reached my outer wall.* Beat. *When he exhaled, his breath shook.*

*His lips crashed onto mine as he slid into me, both of us gasping at the sensation. He pressed his head into the crook of my neck, and he pushed all the way into me. The completeness of lust and friendship consumed me in waves of love and determination to keep him for my own. I'd been on birth control since I was sixteen and didn't want to stop what was happening for one moment.*

*Hips rocked, hitting my clit over and over, pressing and coaxing more pleasure out of me. He lifted his head, his eyebrows knitted. With every slow swirl, my muscles relaxed and let him in farther, slow and splendid. A light kiss to my lips every couple of seconds, our breathing becoming labored. Thrusts getting faster, he touched his lips to mine, open-mouthed, breathing into my soul. He pulsed into me rhythmically but still slow and soft. As he pushed in farther, a shock went right though me. I called out his name in my explosion.*

*I opened my eyes to see his chin up and his mouth open, and he huffed as his body shuddered, his breath hitched and huffed again. He lowered his chin and closed his eyes. His motions were slow, thoughtful, and passionate. His body tensed and shook as he released inside me.*

*He'd lost his battle with himself to have me, to break his rules, he'd chosen me over Gabriella. It didn't matter. He'd leave for the competition circuit, and he'd be back once a year. I needed to break the perpetual cycle.*

*His eyes flew open with a whole bevy of emotions I couldn't place. That look would haunt me for years after. His eyes burned into me. I teared up.*

Don't ever let go, *my mind whispered.*

*I wanted to tell him I loved him. I needed him to stay with me forever. That need was as hollow as my heart. He could never commit to me, and I'd never ask. He needed to tell me he was ready to give up everything to be with me. It wasn't going to happen. Not ever.*

*Jason's a stray dog who didn't belong to me. If I stopped feeding him, he'd stop coming around. That's what I needed to do.*

*We stared at each other, frozen. We both recognized the end.*

*My heart shattered into a thousand pieces. The sooner I accepted it, the sooner I could move on.* Just a little longer, *my heart whimpered. In that moment, he was with me, inside me, breathing into me.*

*A tear dripped down my cheek. He kissed it and held his face to my cheek. He didn't move. His heaving chest felt like he couldn't get enough air. His muscles tightened then relaxed as he breathed in and out, in and out, shaky and agonizing.*

*After what seemed like a silent eternity, he took another deep breath.*

*Not another word was spoken as we fell asleep in each other's arms. When I woke up, he was gone.*

I'd never forget.

## Out Now!

# *What's next on your reading list?*

Champagne Book Group promises to bring to readers fiction at its finest.

Discover your next
fine read!
http://www.champagnebooks.com/

We are delighted to invite you to receive exclusive rewards. Join our Facebook group for VIP savings, bonus content, early access to new ideas we've cooked up, learn about special events for our readers, and sneak peeks at our fabulous titles.

Join now.
https://www.facebook.com/groups/ChampagneBookClub/

Made in the USA
Columbia, SC
11 April 2024

34226969R00098